Broken Gems

By

TJ HAYNES

Published by PHE Ink – Writing Solutions Firm
9597 Jones Rd #213
Houston, TX 77065

PHE Ink and the portrayal of the quill feather are
trademarks of PHE Ink.

The cataloging-in-publication data is on file with the Library
of Congress.

Library of Congress Control Number: 2011910486

ISBN: 978-0-9824475-0-5 Print
ISBN: 978-1-935724-58-2 - eBook

Printed in the United States of America

Printed in 2007 by JL King
Reprinted in 2011 by PHE Ink

Genre: Suspense/Contemporary

Broken Gems is dedicated to the memory of my beloved mother, Barbara Ann Strickland-Haynes.

Throughout my life she has had a profound impact on me and inspired me in immeasurable ways imparting wisdom, guidance, and above else, acceptance and love without condition.

I have been inspired by her strength, and that is illustrated in various scenes and characters throughout this novel.

I've been given a wealth of inspiration to weave the tapestry that became this story.

So, I close with *Vision.*

Vision

I see you
Relentless in your resolve to provide
Protect
Love
Nurture
Often single
Often abused
Neglected
Used
I see you

I see you
Tirelessly working
Overtime
Quality time
All the time
Making ways when none could be seen
Swallowing one's pride
I see you

I see you
In intelligence, strength, and grace
In the laughter of my daughter
In the hands of my grandmother who toiled through decades of strife
Through the seasons of sickness and
In the eyes of my mother closing in death
I see you
Woman of color
Woman of integrity
Woman of pride

Sista... I truly do see you

Acknowledgements

There are several people with whom I'd like to thank for their support while I took on the endeavor of writing this novel. This novel was a labor of love and without the love, kind words, and inspiration from several people, I would not have had the resolve to continue writing.

Mackenzie, my beautiful daughter, I awake every day knowing that it's because of you that I continue to reach for new heights. Mackenzie, you are my muse and my reason for living. I love you, and you inspire me in more ways than I could articulate.

Zachary White, an honest critic, I thank you for your unending support. You've really helped me cross the finish line and encouraged me when I wanted to give up.

Jamal Horsley, you have been behind this project when it was simply a short story. I'm so glad I had your support and motivation.

Monica Joyner and Shanette W. Robinson, you two were pivotal in ensuring that this novel met a successful conclusion; my appreciation is endless.

Regina Petaway, Saara Moye, Lakeesha Johnson, Shawn Blowes and Russell Randall, I thank you for your love and support.

The members of both the Haynes and Strickland families are a collection of dynamic people who encourage me to reach for my goals; and the completion of this novel is just one of many. However, a very special acknowledgement must be given to my brother Terlayne. Terlayne, I could write another novel on how blessed I feel to have you as a brother. However, I'll say this; Mommy must smiling in heaven to see the dynamic of our relationship now. I love you so much, and thank you for your love and unending support.

Last but not least, **TL James** and the entire **PHE Ink Family**. Thank you all for your patience, hard work, and dedication to *Broken Gems*. You all believed in me and my dream. Without you all behind me, Broken Gems wouldn't fly. *Broken Gems* now has her wings and through PHE Ink, the sky is the limit!

My heart is overwhelmed with the amount of support I've received and no matter how often I thank everyone, reading the pages of *Broken Gems*, should serve as evidence of what your love and support has done for me, and I couldn't be more grateful.

Broken Gems

CHAPTER 1

    She was a lover of men and she used them. She used them as though they were as expendable as the cigarette butts she frequently flicked into the air as she drove her drop top S Class Mercedes through the most affluent of neighborhoods. Many would deem her a temptress, a heart breaker, a man-eater, a vixen. Call her what you may, but she was indeed a beauty. She was more captivating than her perfectly sculptured hair and her picturesque body – both have been known to make men careen their cars into oncoming traffic, along with her piercing blue eyes that appeared luminescent in the light. Her beauty was undeniable, even to herself. She walked through life with the notion that the world and everyone in it should take a bow in reverence to her. A woman who embodies this kind of beauty is required to possess a name only fitting for someone who bears the scorn of girlfriends and wives alike: Sapphire.

Sapphire sauntered through the doors of Brooksmen Hall and strolled into lecture hall 3C. As was customary for her, she arrived twenty minutes after the start of class. Was she worried about the ramifications of her tardiness? No. She was used to staying after class and using her feminine "talents" to ensure that she maintained her 4.0 grade point average. Sapphire never concerned herself with the fact that her professors were married men, nor did she care about anything other than what would ultimately benefit her.

When the day's light draws to a close and the eyes of onlookers cease to crawl over her body in admiration, she finally begins to find solace; she escapes from the façade she uses when she steps foot outside of her townhouse. Sapphire is forced to face the demons that no amount of makeup, hair, money, or men could ever take away. She showers in vain, in desperate hopes of washing the pain away; however it doesn't work. At night she nestles her head on her pillow and inconsolably weeps as the memories of her past creep back one by one; nights she desperately wants to and tries to forget...

The sapphire is a beautiful gem; but this Sapphire is damaged... truly damaged. As the semester draws to a close and final exams quickly approach, Sapphire sits in her Advanced Physics class in a daze, hatching the perfect plan. She needs to get ahead, and the best way to do that is to use what God has endowed her with: her undeniable beauty and information that could be used as leverage to destroy the careers and families of many distinguished professionals. Once the clock struck 11:45 A.M., the class was officially over and students rushed out of the room to tackle the rest of their day, all but Sapphire. Sapphire stayed there, sitting, legs crossed with pen in hand, lustfully staring at Professor

Langston. He gave her an inviting nod indicating his wish for her to follow him to his office. She eagerly followed his lead. Once in the privacy of his office, Professor Langston excitedly admits, "I didn't think you were going to show up for class today. I missed you."

"Look, whether you missed me or not, I truly could care less! I need some money! I also don't plan on taking the final. I'm sure you'll be taking care of that," she hissed in a dismissive, snide tone which bewildered the professor.

The professor stood silent for a moment. His mind and heart began to race as thoughts of his career, wife, and child came to mind. Had he made the biggest mistake of his life by allowing sex to trump what took him a lifetime to build? He stood quietly, contemplating how to respond to her demands for money and grades. He knew the leverage she had over him - he would lose everything should she feel it necessary to tell all they had done; the numerous times after class when she would stay and he would "tutor" her on the specifics of force, acceleration, and mass. She was whom he thought of at night; she saturated his mind and made it hard for him to concentrate in her absence from class. It wasn't until this very moment that he really stopped to appreciate the gravity of the situation he'd gotten himself into.

"How much do you need Miss Taylor? I take it there is no way that we can have civility between us?" He could only hope that she would retort with an affirmative answer, but that wouldn't be Sapphire's style.

"Hell no!" she responded in a tenor voice. Her tone indicated that she found satisfaction in what she was about to do to him.

"You have had the pleasure of using my body, and you think that because you gave me a few thousand dollars and a few A's that all is O.K.? Be satisfied knowing that you've had the privilege of touching this. As far as you and I go, it's over. However, you will continue to give me A's whether I show up for class or not, and you will indeed continue to pay me a comfortable stipend on a monthly basis; or let's just say your pretty wife, the Director of Student Affairs, and the President of the University will be told about everything we've done. By the way, I know your daughter attends that prestigious private high school, Wingdom Hall. I would hate for this scandal to surface and for your daughter's life and reputation to be ruined."

Professor Langston knew all too well what needed to be done; now all he needed was the reserve and follow-through to secure the life that he built, making sure that it didn't become destroyed.

"You'll get everything that's coming to you. Now leave my office, Miss Taylor. I know I exercised the poorest judgment, entering into this sordid arrangement with you, and now you threaten to destroy the lives of those I love... my wife, my daughter! I once saw a beautiful woman when I looked at you, now all I see is nothing more than a cheap little slut. Get the hell out... NOW!"

Taken aback by his expression of anger, because she was not accustomed to men exercising any assertiveness with her, she glared and responded, "Just make sure you have my money by Friday, or you know what will happen. Think about that little wife and child of yours." Sapphire grabbed her Gucci handbag and exited the professor's office.

While driving, Sapphire realizes, yet again, that she is going home alone. The only numbers in her cell phone are those of professors that she sleeps with for grades and those who provide her with the lifestyle that she feels is befitting for a woman of her beauty. Alone... she is always alone. She has no friends; women deem her toxic and men view her as nothing more than a personification of vanity; one to be used for their temporary enjoyment, not to bring home to meet the family. To most, she is seen as entirely devoid of any substance.

She arrives to an empty home where she has no one to dialogue with, except for her inner demons. She bathes in a shower large enough to fit several adults, allowing the warm air of her townhouse to dry her body naturally. She tries not to let her mind become adrift, letting memories of her past float back to the present, but her efforts are to no avail. She stands in front of her mirror in a daze. She is taken back several years to when she was a girl, ten years old. Sapphire never knew her father and her mother always worked two jobs to ensure that the rent was paid. There were times when Sapphire's mother could not afford to maintain the utilities, so at any given time the lights or the heat were turned off. This is the life that Sapphire was accustomed to; her youth and innocence blinded her to the severity of her situation. The following year, when she turned eleven, her mother began dating and fell in love with a man who proved to shape Sapphire's life in profound ways - she loved this man. He was the father that she never had. However, she never knew that he had a past and lived a lifestyle that would contaminate her life and irreparably damage her.

Sapphire's mother allowed her love for her boyfriend to cloud her judgment, and she experimented with what started out as recreational drug use. Sapphire, who once received unyielding attention from her mother, noticed the attention she once received was becoming less and less frequent. Her mother's presence in the home became almost non-existent. One day, upon arrival home from school, Sapphire was greeted by her teary-eyed mother delivering the news that the man whom she loved was murdered. This was Sapphire's first exposure to death, and she received no parental comfort; instead she received a mother who became a shell of the woman she once was. Her mother would tell her how beautiful she was, and how "Pa-Pa" always mirrored the same sentiment. The compliments would come in plentifully, but her mother would become increasingly detached from Sapphire's world. The innocent world she once knew began to take on many shades of gray. She found herself becoming angry and always longing for something she couldn't quite explain.

The morning of January 9th, Sapphire's birthday, she awoke shivering; a chill that was all too familiar. She tried to turn on the lamp, but the only light she would receive was from the flashlight she kept hidden under her bed and the street lights that glowed through the bed sheets that were used as curtains. She glanced at her watch and noticed that it was just past 3 A.M. She stumbled into her living room to find her mother on the couch in a compromising position with a man. Startled at the sight, she ran back to her room and jumped into her bed. All she could do was cry. How did her life take such a downward spiral? Could things become any worse?

The following night, while Sapphire was in her room trying to drift off to sleep, she heard the voices of two men and her mother in heated discussion.

"I know I owe you, but I already gave you all my jewelry and you know what we did last night. Just tell me what else you want!"

The male voice, seemingly unmoved by the pleading tone of the mother, retorted quickly and forcefully. Sapphire snuck to her bedroom door and opened it slightly to see what was going on.

"Your daughter! She's a sweet looking young thang. I know she's fresh too... I know we can have some fun with that. We can consider all the debts cleared. If she is half as good as you are then I know it'll be worth it. Yo, you already saw what happened when your boy neglected to own up and pay what he owed." Sapphire watched the man take out a syringe and a bag from his coat, then toss them on the ground. Her mother looks at the two men, and begins to cry.

"Just don't damage her face..."

Sapphire, after realizing the gravity of what is going on, tries to escape out of her window; but it is too late. One of the men grabs her and throws her to the floor. In the coldness of the night, all that can be seen are the silhouettes of men annihilating the innocence she has left, and the spark of a lighter from the other room.

As Sapphire awakes from her daze, alone and naked in her townhouse, she notices that the doorbell has been ringing. She quickly dresses in a silk robe and answers the door.

"What the hell are you doing here?" she snaps. "You've got some fucking nerve coming to my home unannounced," she seethes with her voice rising, and her agitation growing more and more by the second.

Before another word could be uttered by Sapphire, a knife was forced into her chest and abdomen in several swift, consecutive motions. Sapphire fell to the floor and the unannounced guest left as quickly as they had arrived

Once the news of Sapphire Taylor's death began to travel amongst the students on the campus of the University, questions began to swirl. Her personal life began to be scrutinized, and rumors were dissected for their percentage of truth. Discussion of the homes she had destroyed ran rampant, and her personality was torn to shreds. Noticeably absent from the conversations about the death of Sapphire was any sorrow... any outward display of grief over the loss of human life. She held no value to anyone. She was a loner; she never allowed anyone to breach the walls she built around herself when she was young. She never learned to let go.

The night of the murder, Professor Langston arrived home around 3 A.M. He was flushed, pale, and ready to confess his sins to a wife who was anxiously awaiting his arrival. He had been driving around aimlessly for several hours thinking of what he had done. He tried to figure out exactly how he would alleviate his soul and atone for his terrible and unforgivable lapse in judgment for doing the unforgivable…

When Professor Langston arrived home, there was a letter taped to his garage. Shaking, he exits the car, retrieves the letter, and returns to the warmth of his Mercedes. He hesitates before reading it, assuming that it was left there to bear bad tidings. How much more could he take? He decided to read the letter before entering the house; before he laid the weight of his burdens upon his wife; before he plead to her in desperation in order to salvage the family that he was hoping would not dessert him. When he opened the envelope, he recognized the familiar handwriting:

Daddy,

Please forgive me. There is quite a bit you don't know; quite a bit I haven't shared with you and Mommy. I've been dating this guy named Jonathan Torres for the past year. He is older than me. Daddy, I wanted to tell you and Mommy but I knew you would freak out. Jonathan works as a Mortgage Broker and is the youngest broker at his brokerage company; he's 26 years old. I know he's 9 years older than me, but I truly do love him.

Everything was going great between the two of us, that is, until one night while working on my calculus homework at his condo, he happened to leave his checkbook on the kitchen table. He usually leaves his checkbook in the nightstand, so I decided return it to its proper place. When I picked it up, a check fell out, signed and dated for the amount of $3500.00, made payable to a Sapphire Taylor. The memo line read: "Townhouse payment".

Daddy, I was completely confused. I wanted to know who this Sapphire Taylor was, why he was writing a check to her for that amount of money, and why he was giving it to her for a townhouse; people are supposed to give him money; he's the Mortgage Broker! Also, the name sounded so familiar to me. Then, it finally dawned on me where I knew the name. When we took a trip to your school, and received a tour from one of our previous graduates, she told many of us about the "dirt" at the University. She mentioned Sapphire and her rumored addiction to men, and her sordid relationships to different professors. Why would Jonathan be giving this skank money? Well, Daddy, I am your daughter and you've always taught me that "the solution to any question ends with active investigation". So I followed him one night. I followed him to the townhouse of this Sapphire Taylor. Daddy, he's been cheating on me with this whore. How could he do this to me? I told Mommy, and she confided in me that she believes the Sapphire I was talking about is the same Sapphire that your secretary's daughter said that you were having an affair with!

We've known about you and your slut for quite some time now. That woman is poison! You've been sleeping with her, Jonathan slept with her, and she's been blackmailing him; God only knows who else she's got her hooks in. I just couldn't take it any longer. She's threatened to destroy our family, and not only that, she has come in-between me and the man I love. Mommy hides her pain differently than me. She can pretend as if everything is o.k., but I can't. I refuse. I also learned another lesson from you: "Protect your family at all costs! Self-preservation is the number-one human instinct." Well, I wasn't given any choice. Daddy, I had to protect myself from the woman who didn't even know me, but was set out to destroy me. So I went to her house. She knew exactly who I was without me even introducing myself. I can't believe how condescending this woman was. She gave me attitude and she was extorting money from my father and boyfriend. She's been sleeping with the two men in my life. That bitch had to be stopped! Before I knew it, I was stabbing her... Daddy, I wanted her dead, but I didn't think I'd actually go through with it. I just wanted to scare her -

threaten her to leave all of us alone and prey on someone else; but it was the look in her eyes; that cold unrepentant look just sent me into a complete frenzy.

Daddy, when the police find out what I did, I know everything I've worked for will be lost, and I will have disgraced the family. I'm so sorry. Please tell Mommy. I can't face her or you.

I love you,

When the Professor finished reading the note, his heart was atremble and he was searching for breath. Was he dreaming? Did he just read that his only child had committed the heinous murder of his mistress? His wife lay in bed, waiting for his arrival, and he was left with a heavy choice to make. What to do? Raindrops began to fall upon the windshield of his car as he contemplated his options, and he tried to dissect the course of events that lead to this catastrophic night. He reached into his pocket and pulled out his cellular phone.

"911, what is your emergency?" The voice on the line answered.

"My name is Gregory Langston, and I just committed a murder..."

CHAPTER 2

The life one leads as a wife of a respected professor can prove to be a lonely one, especially when she is encouraged not to utilize the degrees in which she worked so hard to acquire. Joan Langston only bore one child before losing the ability to have children. She had to undergo a hysterectomy to remove the cysts developing in her ovaries. Joan fancied herself the quintessential housewife; she not only bore the primary responsibilities of parenting her only child, but she also had to maintain an estate that was coined her husband's showpiece, a place where he could be proud to bring his colleagues. She perfected her cooking and developed a palate for exotic herbs and spices that she used to impress the guests they entertained. She worked out regularly to ensure that her body was toned to her husband's liking. She always thought back to the words her mother whispered in her ear on her wedding day, "Baby, you are a vision. Now listen to your dear Mother - mark my words. Whatever you did to get this man, you better continue doing to keep him..."

Joan, as evident through the women in her family, was predisposed to being on the heavier side. She always worked extremely hard to maintain a svelte figure. Her routine consisted of five miles of jogging daily and light weight training. Her body was that of someone several years her junior. She maintained flawless skin in part to a strict skincare regimen. She maintained a clear belief that she was indeed a reflection of her husband. Her hair care regimen was just as strict as both her skin and workout routines. She benefitted from her Native American ancestry and was fortunate enough to have the hair type that her husband found appealing. She could wear her hair either curly or straight to the pleasure of her husband because it never looked "ethnic". He fancied long hair, so she never cut it, even though for many years she longed to.

Sexually, Joan can be considered by any definition to be a "freak". Joan learned early on in her marriage what only a married woman would be privy to know; the art of how to win an Academy Award without actually bringing home the trophy. She would perform sexual acts with her husband that she found to be vile. However, she would carry them out with vigor and eagerness; making him believe that she thoroughly enjoyed every sexual encounter, no matter how tasteless, inconsiderate, or bad the timing was. For example, when she was healing from her hysterectomy, he wanted to be pleased orally. She obliged to ensure that her husband's needs were met.

For the vast majority of Joan's twenty-three year marriage to Professor Langston, she found herself lost in the tedium of life. She lost herself in pleasing a man she cherished and loved more than she did herself. She grew to view her inability to have children as a weakness; it was a flaw which caused her to feel the need to overcompensate for the one thing that she knew she would never be able to give him. She only had few outlets, one being a secret she held close to her chest; she never divulged it to anyone, not even those she loved most in life. Joan also viewed her daughter, Anna, as a cherished outlet, and then there was her beloved neighbor, Jason.

As Joan went through her normal routine of cleaning her house, her cell phone rang. She pressed the button on her Bluetooth. "Hello."

"*How you doing*?" Jason questioned with his best Wendy Williams imitation.

"I'm splendid, J, couldn't be better." Joan expressed with a note of friendly sarcasm.

"I've been meaning to call you, but you know Dr. Stevens has been keeping me busy lately," he recounted in a tone that indicated that he wanted her to pursue a line of questioning.

"You mean Christopher?"

"Yes, but I like to call him a Doctor. Doesn't that word just sound good rolling off the tongue? Doctor? Doctor... Doctor!" he moaned with a boisterous laugh.

"I guess. But listen, I'd love to hear about your multiple-hour romp with Christopher, however, I have to get this house dusted and finish my hair. I'm trying to make sure that things are perfect for Greg tonight."

"Joan, why do you put yourself out there like that for him? Girl, you only got one life to live, so when are you going to start to live it for you? Your daughter is about to move out and you're there with him; I notice how his car is not always in the driveway at night..."

Abruptly Joan interrupted Jason, "Look, I know you didn't call me to discuss whether or not my husband comes home at night. What you can do for me is this: come over and help me flat iron my hair. I know he loves it when my hair is bone-straight. I just want to make things special. So, will you come?"

Sucking his teeth, he responded, "Yeah, just let me freshen up. I still have Dr. Stevens all over me," he said with a chuckle. "While I'm working on your mop, I'll fill you in on my rendezvous with *DOCTOR* STEVENS."

Jason always proved to be a comfort to Joan, even though many times his candor dealt a mighty blow to her already fragile ego. His words of encouragement sometimes afforded her the time to reflect over her life and think about what life might be like if things were different: if her husband were more attentive, if her husband would only show her that he loved her for who she was and didn't make her feel like a possession. When Jason arrived at the Langston estate, he helped Joan with the remaining dusting and began to flat iron her hair. Jason was well-versed with hair care; it was a trade he acquired to help bring him extra money while he was in college. While sectioning Joan's hair and applying the Indian Hemp Hair Oil to her scalp and hair, he began to fill Joan's ears with details of his encounter with the gorgeous Dr. Stevens.

"We were just going to watch a movie and I was supposed to give him a massage; but that is seriously not what ended up happening. You know how fine that man is... Well, I don't know what got into him, but let me tell you, the movie was watching *us*. The second I turned the movie on, I turn around, and there he is, right behind me. He grabbed my waist and kissed me. Usually, I ask that he take a shower before we do anything intimate, but there was something about how he grabbed me. I couldn't open my mouth to express the words. I became totally lost in him. Damn! The way his hands were grabbing me - it felt like it was the first time he had ever been with a man. He was so strong and forceful. He pushed me against the wall, grabbed both of my hands, and held them over my head with one of his. He unfastened my belt and the button on my pants with his other hand. You can just imagine what happened next. He was stern with me… like a drill sergeant in the army. He commanded me to do things to him, and like a good soldier, I followed his every command."

Listening to Jason tell his story made Joan uncomfortable - not because it was a story of two men engaging in sexual acts, but because she found herself jealous of her best friend. She longed to have the experience of not living a life carrying around the insecurities and burdens she felt that she would never rid herself of. To not illustrate her ever-growing jealousy, she interjected a joke into his story. "Is it getting hot in here, or is it just me? *Lord*," she uttered, fanning herself.

"Girl, that's not even the best part. When we got to the bedroom, he purposely turned off the air conditioner and told me to lie down on the bed. Again, I did as I was told. While lying there, he crawled on the bed and looked into my eyes. His honey-colored eyes were gazing into mine - he'd just stare at me and kiss on my body. Every time I'd try to grab for him or touch him at all, he'd slap my hands away. He wanted total control. His kisses began at my lips, but found their way south, below the equator. After a while, I exploded… and let's just say that there was no mess to clean up. Girl, I thought I saw an angel in Heaven! It was so *good*!

Joan's mind became adrift as Jason continued to recall his rendezvous in explicit detail.

"That man's mouth is a blessing. However, he wasn't anywhere near done with me; he grabbed me and pulled me into a long deep kiss with remnants of me still lingering in his mouth. He instructed me to 'taste him', so it was my turn to demonstrate some skill. Girl, his caramel body looked like the epitome of perfection as it glistened off of the flickering light from the candle on my nightstand. Every lick made his muscles flex. That man is so very gifted. I don't know what they feed those boys in the south, but I *do* know that I want to thank his momma! When he could no longer take what I was doing to him below his equator, he commanded me to turn over on my stomach. Let's just say things did not end until several hours later."

Joan was slightly jealous, and yet she was slightly excited by eagerly anticipating the night with her husband. "Thanks for making me want my husband even more!" she exclaimed jokingly.

"You almost done?"

"Yep, just wanna get the kitchen."

"So you had a wonderful night; I know I plan on having one tonight. I'm going to be waiting for Greg, and when he walks in the door, he's going to be truly surprised to see what I have in store for him."

"What are you going to wear?"

"Well, I have this black dress in mind, but I want your opinion on how it looks once I put it on."

"That's what I'm here for, besides being here to brag about my DOCTOR... Did I mention how big it is? *How you doing?* You're all set, girl. Let's see what this dress looks like."

"You are so damn crazy." Joan said with a friendly laugh.

While trying on the black dress she initially intended to wear to impress her husband, Joan and Jason talked more about his growing fondness for Dr. Stevens and how Jason truly wished to see her happy. Jason hoped her night would be as beautiful and freaky as his was the night before. Finally, they collectively decided on a dress: a black Dior dress that she "forgot" she even owned price tag still intact. Jason found it while he was joking with her about stealing one of her husband's suits.

"Girl... it's a bit short, but if you want to make a statement, this dress will do it. Since when do you wear Dior?

She looked at the dress momentarily, studying it, trying to remember when she bought it. "I don't even remember buying it - I must have picked it up on one of those days when I was out binge shopping." She tried to convince herself of the words she spoke, but she knew deep inside that she had never purchased the garment. If she indicated the truth, Jason would have never let the situation rest. She had to keep focused on her objective for the evening: giving her husband a night he wouldn't forget. The dress was a great fit, and to her astonishment, it complimented her body quite well. "I do look good in this, huh?"

"If I were straight, your husband would be in trouble."

"Boy if I weren't married, and if Christopher, oh excuse me, Dr. Stevens has the skill you say, and was straight, you'd be in trouble and really mad at me!" She said laughing.

"Look bitch, don't get cut!" Jason shot back giving her a kiss on the cheek.

"Greg should be home in a few minutes. Let me light the candles and get the rest of his surprise ready. I'll fill you in tomorrow. Thank you for everything, J."

"No problem. Have a great night with the hubby, and do everything that I would do, plus sixty nine more!" As she walked him to the door, she tried to put the fact that she was wearing a dress that was not her own into the back of her mind. This night was about her and her husband.

Joan was expecting Greg to arrive home within the next twenty minutes. One hour passed and there was no call, no text message - nothing. She called him, only to have the call go straight to his voicemail. The first hour turned into two, then two to three. Joan sat on the couch trying to maintain her composure, trying to understand why her husband would not be considerate enough to at least give her a phone call. She knew within her heart why, but again, she wanted to push those thoughts to the back of her mind. She then began to blow out the candles that were strategically placed around the house to create a seductive ambiance to aid her quest at seduction. She ascended the stairs and went to the bedroom, reached into a storage box underneath her bed, and took out an envelope that was sent to her two weeks prior with no return address. She reopened the envelope and gazed at its contents. The words prompted a river of tears to flow, like water gushing from a broken levee. Although she tried to ignore her thoughts, once again, she knew her husband wouldn't be coming home… at least not tonight.

CHAPTER 3

As much as Joan wanted to reach out to her daughter, to hug her, to tell her that everything would be o.k., she simply remained silent. Joan's relationship with her daughter, Anna, and her maternal authority over her child was always usurped by Professor Langston's dominance. The walls of their lavish estate could tell many stories; stories that highlighted the consequences of when misogynistic, disparaging, and controlling language fall in succession, landing on a victim, and leaving in its wake a broken spirit, anger, frustration, and a rising sense of loss. The inhabitants that dwelled within the Langston home traversed a rocky sea of emotions; however Anna was not exempt from feeling the stinging blow from the pain of growing up a Langston.

Being the product of two well-educated parents, Anna shouldered the pressures from her father to finish high school as the valedictorian. Both Professor Langston and his wife were named valedictorian of their high school classes, and he wanted to ensure that his only child would follow suit. He would monitor her use of the Internet by installing monitoring software to her laptop; he'd limit her cellular phone activity, restrict the amount of television she was allowed to watch, and he handpicked all of the extra-curricular activities she participated in. He always sensed resistance in his daughter, but ignored it as he maintained the final say in all matters in his home. When he was not around to act as the enforcer, Joan was designated to carry on with the rules he laid forth.

At seventeen years old, Anna Langston would be what many in the 'hood' would refer to as a "dime". She possessed looks that made her classmates envious. Her eyes were naturally grey, and she had hair like that of her mother: long and deemed beautiful by most standards of beauty. Her skin always appeared soft and delicate. In complexion, Anna followed the likes of Halle Berry, Jada Pinkett-Smith, and Beyonce. Her skin possessed hints of red, displaying traits from her mother's American Indian ancestry. Anna didn't have to wear makeup as her beauty shone naturally. With all of her beauty and intelligence, both in school and at home, she felt alone and she also felt a need to keep her guard up. Like her mother, Anna only had few outlets to her mundane existence. Her most valued outlet was her boyfriend, Jonathan, and she kept their relationship a secret from her parents for more than a year.

The day Anna long had been dreading approached; the senior class rankings would be announced. She had no doubt that she would rank at the top of her class - but there was some doubt as to whether or not she would edge out her biggest competitor, Angela McFadden, who happened to be the daughter of one of her father's colleagues. Anna maintained the highest averages in all of her classes with the exception of one, where she faltered and received an A-, in her Advanced

Placement Calculus course. She entered the school feeling the weight of the world on her shoulders - or was it the weight of her father's demands for perfection?

The seniors were called down to the auditorium during the final period of the day to be given their class ranks. Student names were called by the class advisors and guidance counselors, and a plethora of moans came from unhappy students and joyous chatter could be heard from students who knew that their hard work had paid off. Absent from the reverberations of student banter was Anna's voice. She stood transfixed on the number placed on the paper in her trembling hands. She was immobile; she thought of the countless hours that she was denied the opportunity to experience a life that her classmates took for granted. She knew that the paper that she held in her hands sealed her fate and would cause icy winds to blow once she arrived home. She was ready. She was tired. Anna, in this moment of introspection looking at the paper, vowed to never again allow anyone or anything to stand in her way. Anna's private moment was interrupted by Angela peering over her shoulder. "Number 2, huh? I guess you couldn't pull it off after all; huh, Anna? I'm sure your daddy will be so very proud of you!" she hissed with a note of chilling sarcasm.

"Look, right now is not the time."

"When would be the right time? At graduation when you deliver your speech after I deliver mine? Oh, wait! How about when we take our pictures for the yearbook, and I take mine before yours seeing as how I edged you out for the top spot? Or how about when my father is bragging to your father about how you couldn't even pull it together in a class like AP Calculus? We all know math isn't your subject; couldn't you get a tutor or something?"

"Bitch, I'm warning you, if you don't back the fuck out my face and leave me alone, one of us will leave this auditorium injured and it sure as hell won't be me."

"*Wow*, such harsh words! Looks like someone needs anger management. I guess I'd better leave you to your sobbing while I go celebrate my status. By the way, Number 2, tell your mother I said 'hello' - you two have more in common than I thought."

"What the fuck is that supposed to mean?"

"Well, a husband and wife are supposed to be equals. We all know your mother is nothing more than your father's maid; and from what I hear, she's not even number 1 in his book. It's sad when a wife will play second fiddle to her husband's slutty students. Two dumb bitches..."

"I fucking warned you, bitch..."

Before Angela could fully turn around to walk away, Anna dropped the paper containing her class ranking and grabbed the back of Angela's head with her left hand and punched Angela's face with her right hand. The hit was such a release for Anna that she struck her again; this time knocking Angela to the floor. The force of Anna's punches dazed Angela - but Anna was nowhere near done with her assault. She climbed on top of her and began to punch and claw at her face like a wild woman. Angela's attempts at trying to protect her face were futile. The shrill screams from Angela alerted both the faculty and students. As two male guidance counselors pulled a kicking and screaming Anna off of a bloodied and battered Angela, the consequences of the day that Anna dreaded had only begun to come to fruition.

CHAPTER 4

As Anna waited outside of Principal Mackenzie's office, she sat stone-faced, staring at photos hanging on the wall. The photos illustrated different moments of student achievement. One photo caught her attention; it was a photo of her accepting an award during her junior year for having completed a rigorous course of study in forensics at the local university, which afforded her college credit. She appeared so happy in that photo; she could see her parents in the background beaming from ear to ear, proud of their only child's accomplishment. She knew that momentarily her mother would exit the Principal's office; she would have to explain her actions and take personal accountability for what transpired. She wished she could slow the hands of time and prolong the torturous ride home, but her wish did not come true. Her mother exited Principal Mackenzie's office with a pale look on her face. "Thank you for your time, and for being so lenient. Trust me; I will handle Anna when I get home." She shook his hand and gestured for Anna to follow her lead to the car.

To break the deafening silence between them, Anna decided to be the first to speak. "Mom, I know you're upset with me, but you know how the McFaddens are, and Angela was warned. I told her to leave me alone, but she wouldn't, so she got what was coming to her."

"Ten days. *Ten fucking days,* Anna! You know damn well what is going to happen when your father gets home. What the hell could have caused you to lose control to the point where you break her nose, blacken both her eyes, and cut her face?"

"She was gloating about out-ranking me."

"She *beat* you? Oh my *God!*" Joan sat there, agonizing, knowing that her home would erupt in more ways than she could imagine when Gregory arrived home. He placed so much importance on the image his family projected. The 'horrible' news that his daughter, who was not only named salutatorian, but who was also being suspended from school, would cause a volcano to erupt. She didn't know if she possessed the power to quell its explosion.

"Mom, I did my best and it wasn't good enough. You always said giving my best was the most important thing. Daddy, on the other hand, is a completely different story. She just kept on taunting me and taunting me. I tried to get her to leave me alone, but she wouldn't. Then she began to talk about Daddy... and you."

"What'd she say?"

"Ma, you don't want to know."

"What the hell did she say, Anna?"

"She talked about how you're weak, how you let Daddy run all over you, and how you basically turn a blind eye to him sleeping around with his students. Then she ended with calling us both 'stupid bitches'."

Like a deer caught in headlights, Joan kept her eyes on the road and she drove silently for the remainder of the ride home. Her silence spoke volumes. This was the first time words were ever vocalized between the two of them about Gregory's infidelity. She wished she could shelter her daughter from knowing the hard truth, but she knew of no way to do so. She hoped her silence over the years would be enough; but the intelligence of an incredibly a gifted girl and the resonance of the adage, 'what's done in the dark shall come to light' rang true. Upon arrival to the house, the only other words spoken came from Joan. "Go ahead to your room. I'll do my best to explain things to your father when he gets home. I am disappointed - not because of your class ranking, but because you chose to whip her ass in school. You should have waited until you saw that little bitch in the street." She then kissed her daughter on the forehead and went to her room to pray for the strength to get through the storm that she knew would come.

At 2 A.M., Anna awakened to the sounds of her mother and father engaging in the most heated argument she had ever heard in her seventeen years of life. She was accustomed to her father dominating every aspect of life at the Langston home, but tonight, she heard her mother's voice.

"You walk in here at 1:30 in the morning and then you want to wake our daughter up just to yell at her about not meeting your expectations? Are you fucking *serious*? Why don't you just go back to wherever the hell you just came from? She knows, Greg, and if your ass had any fucking class you would at least be discreet - at least then your business wouldn't be in the street." Joan yelled with a voice Anna didn't think her mother possessed.

"This is *my* fucking house - *I* pay the bills and *I* will do as *I* please. *I* come and go as *I* please. If she's a fuck up, which *clearly* she is, you'd better trust and believe I'm going to let her know. She couldn't even out-rank a McFadden. With your blood running through her veins, it doesn't surprise me."

"You son-of-a-*bitch*!"

"And don't worry about my 'business being in the street'. Until you, or anyone else has concrete evidence of anything, then its only rumor - nothing else. However, what that *is* true is that my wife can't give me a real family and my daughter has proven to be just as big of a disappointment as her barren mother!" he roared with disdain over his wife's attempt at being assertive.

Joan hoped that there was still some shred, some semblance of the man she once loved and adored within her husband. She hoped that somewhere within the man she married was a good person, but tonight his words destroyed that hope. This night, Joan Elizabeth Langston grew numb.

Professor Langston then stormed into Anna's room. "Get the hell out the bed! How the *fuck* could you embarrass me like this and get suspended, nonetheless not out-rank a McFadden?"

Infuriated at overhearing the way he had just spoken to her mother, Anna responded in a way that demonstrated the side of herself that lay dormant; but was released when she was handed her freedom on a single piece of paper... #2. Pandora's Box was now open and she never wanted it to close again. No one could close it, not even the powerful Professor Langston. She retorted to her father sarcastically, "I'm not in the mood to deal with you right now. What you should be doing is apologizing to your wife."

"What did you say to me?" he questioned, moving closer to her in disbelief.

"I said, you should be apologizing to your wife, she's in the bathroom crying because of you."

"Your mother is not important right now. What I want is for you to explain how you could embarrass me like this. After all I've done for this family - after all I've done for you - and this is the payment I get? Getting suspended because you can't take the heat from a McFadden? You're just as weak as your mother!"

"Weak? How can you stand there and call anyone weak when you're the one who has to make himself feel like a man by fucking women half his age? Without me and Mommy to make you look good, you'd be nothing more than a lonely, middle-aged college professor who fucks his students."

Those words were smashed back into her mouth by her father's open hand. Anna's body crumbled under the weight of her father's blow. "You dare to talk to me like that in my own house, girl? You see how far you get without my help. I'm done with you. When you are ready to apologize, I'll be waiting." Seconds after he exited her room, Anna heard the sound of the front door slam closed.

While lying on the floor holding her face, Anna had an epiphany: *change is inevitable, growth is optional*. She needed to grow - and in order for her to grow, *genuinely* grow, she needed to make it happen herself. She knew exactly what she needed to do.

CHAPTER 5

Poverty can be seen as a beast that viciously attacks its victim, forcing it to either fight for its survival or succumb under its control. Those from privileged homes will never know the cruelties one must endure when poverty creeps in and taints the innocence of a young girl's life. Sapphire learned many hard lessons as a child, but none harder than when her body lay limp on the floor the day after her 12th birthday. Her mother spoke words that were inaudible to her. Lying there she wished her body was numb, that she couldn't feel the pain from being completely brutalized by two strangers. Her throat felt raw from her futile attempts at screaming, and her naked body was chafed in numerous places from the friction of the cheap carpeting. Her vagina and anus felt as if they both were aflame. She could still feel the pain, and blood seeped from both. Why was her mother talking?

What was she saying? What could she say? As she tried to muster the strength to get up, she collapsed under the weight of her injuries, and lost consciousness.

Sapphire awoke in unfamiliar surroundings; she was in a comfortable bed that had fresh linen. She didn't know where she was. She was far too weak to give in to the anxiety that she felt, but she did sit up in the bed and she made an attempt at trying to walk - but again she failed. Luckily, she had the cushion of the bed beneath her. The voice of an elderly woman startled her. "Baby, you had some kind of terrible night, didn't you? That mother of yours left the door wide open again. I found you on the floor."

"Who are you?" Sapphire spoke in a hoarse whisper.

"I'm Ms. Strickland, from a few doors down," she said. She came closer to Sapphire, taking a seat next to her on the bed. "See, I've lived in this building for more than 40 years, and I keep to myself. I don't want no trouble with the element that comes in and out of here."

"So, you know what happened then?"

"Yes baby, I know. It's a damn shame too. Just because some women push out babies don't mean that they should be given the title of 'mother'. I've seen it too many times."

"I know she didn't mean it. She couldn't have."

"Child, this will probably be one of the hardest lessons you will have to learn in life, but Ms. Strickland is gonna teach it to you. You can't depend on people for shit, you hear me? People will let you down every time - guaranteed. Look at your mother. Baby, I know everything that goes on in this building, and trust me, I could write a book. You have to make your own way in this here life. If you want something, take it. Don't let anyone or anything get in your way; just make it happen, baby."

"It hurts so bad." she sobbed inconsolably into Ms. Strickland's arm.

"I have a feeling you'll be just fine. You can stay here with me. I have a feeling your mother won't be back. Them drugs gotta hold of her. I've seen it too many times, baby. When a mother gives up her own baby, there ain't nothing but the good Lord that can turn things around - and she don't strike me as the type that is seeking Him anytime soon."

The two sat in silence. Ms. Strickland rocked Sapphire as she cried and purged her soul of its troubles. She needed this night. Ms. Strickland's heart provided Sapphire with the comfort she needed to get through the most troubling time of her childhood. She needed to feel that there was an adult that would be there to help her see through the midst; to make sense of events that defy explanation and to provide hope, hope that the future wasn't going to be bleak. Sapphire's eyes closed; her heart was still heavy, her soul still weeping, and her life still in a wreck. However, in Ms. Strickland's arms, she did acquire a silver lining to the cloud hovering over her life. All no longer seemed completely lost.

CHAPTER 6

Irony is when someone shows genuine tenderness during times of weakness so that life can begin anew. Two months after Sapphire's rape, she awoke to the smell of bacon frying in the kitchen. As she stretched, she thought about how her life now mirrored the lives of children she saw on television; children who had stability; children who had a parental figure who provided the necessities of life. She was now guaranteed three meals a day and she didn't have to rely on pilfering lunches from school to mitigate the all too common hunger pains that had been known to keep her awake at night. It was a bright Sunday morning, and Sapphire knew after breakfast that it would be time for her to get dressed and go to church; this was a new endeavor for her, but it was something she found, even at 12 years old, to be quite pleasing.

As wonderful as Sapphire found her new life living with Ms. Strickland, she found it necessary to master the art of hiding her feelings from her new guardian out of fear of seeming ungrateful. While in the seclusion of her bedroom, she would fixate on the one photo she had of her mother. The photo brought a floodgate of emotions to the forefront of her consciousness. She still felt love for her mother - she longed for her presence. She also was pained by the reality that her mother was the root of all of her troubles; but absent from the emotions she'd experienced was anger. Sapphire never knew that feeling; she longed, she knew hurt and disappointment intimately, but anger was not in her repertoire.

Nights for Sapphire proved to be the time that troubled her the most. During the day, she would busy herself in school, soaking up as much knowledge as humanly possible. She'd read books, ask for extra work from her teachers, and volunteer to do extra chores around the house. One would never know that she fell victim to such horrific acts, acts that haunted her nightly. She busied herself, trying to purge her mind from reliving the destruction of her innocence, from hearing her vaginal walls rip, from feeling the manhood of two different men plunging in and out of all of her available orifices without any regard to her pain or tears. She wanted to forget the smell of their sweat, but she couldn't. She wanted to forget the scent of alcohol, tobacco, and marijuana that clung to the beasts. That stench obliterated her self-worth, her childhood, and her ability to feel comfort around those of the opposite gender, but she couldn't. She'd awake in the middle of the night, panting, covered in sweat, and terrified. She was too ashamed to tell anyone, even Ms. Strickland. She figured if she continued to pray, things would turn around. Things had to get better; God already sent her Ms. Strickland.

CHAPTER 7

There are many lessons to be learned about life when one attends high school. It's more than a time when one makes a transition from adolescence into young adulthood. High school is a time where decisions are made about the direction in which one's future will go. From a social aspect, memories are built that remain throughout the rest of one's life. Milestones are crossed and the foundation is built for future success. Sapphire, while in high school, was rather introverted. She remained steadfast in her belief that the memories of her past would fade with prayer. She was resolute, and her senior year of high school had come quicker than she had expected. The years living with Ms. Strickland provided her with many comforts; however, she still suffered in silence.

Throughout the years, Ms. Strickland tried to encourage her to "get out the house more" and "date a little", but Sapphire had no interest. She felt uncomfortable around the opposite sex. She primarily kept to herself. She did, however, catch the attention from those around her. The looks her mother had once been so proud of had blossomed and were passed on to her daughter, now that Sapphire was reaching young adulthood. While at church, she noticed lengthy stares from the male patrons, and the growing resentful stares from the women who began to treat her with contempt, but she paid it little attention. Sapphire's life focused around obtaining knowledge and seeking help from God. She was only interested in things that helped her to fight the demons that wrestled for control over her sanity when the sun went down, during the times she lay in solitude. She'd been fighting this battle for years; thus far the battle had been a stalemate.

Ecstatic over the grades she received on her first senior year report card, Sapphire rushed home to Ms. Strickland to share that she again managed to score straight A's. She loved to see the glow on Ms. Strickland's face whenever she accomplished feats that defied her horrific past. Over the years Ms. Strickland had become a mother to her in every sense of the word. She nurtured her, cared for her, and provided the structure and balance in her life that was needed in order for her to survive. She truly loved her. She was indeed her savior. While she still held space in her heart for her birth mother, Ms. Strickland filled the emptiness left by her mother's departure. Upon arriving home, Sapphire ran to Ms. Strickland's room. There, she came across her new mother sitting upright on her bed with a look on her face that she'd never seen before. Before Sapphire could even utter a word, she was waved over to have seat.

"Momma, what's wrong?"

"Baby, there is something that I can no longer hide from you. You are old enough to know the truth; I fear you'll find out soon enough. From the first day you came to live with me I tried to instill in you faith in the good Lord. I need for you to trust in him now."

"You're scaring me. What's wrong? Did something happen?"

"Baby, I'm not much longer for this life. I've been battling cancer for many years. I've been in remission for quite some time. Unfortunately, I didn't quite hit that seven year mark. My last visit to my oncologist showed that not only did my cancer return, but it has also now spread to my stomach and liver," Ms. Strickland spoke softly as tears began to roll down her face. She tried to remain strong, but her strength was fading. "They want me to undergo chemo, but baby, I'm too damn old. God is telling me - it's my time. My time's coming to rest my head on The Maker's shoulders. Lord knows I don't want to leave you here, but I trust you'll do what's right."

Sapphire sat motionless, unable to move. She knew all too well what to expect when cancer attacked the human body. It leaves a path of destruction in its wake; it leaves its mark on the lives of those who are unfortunate enough to see its destruction. There were no tears; all she could do was question, "Why?"

"Baby, God has his plan. It's not for us to question why. We just have to trust in it, and believe that things will work out accordingly."

"What am I going to do without you?"

"Live baby… live…"

The two sat there holding each other, the weight of the news touching each of them differently. One, thinking about the impending doom: the suffering, the pain, what death must be like, faith, God, or whether there is a God, Sapphire, and what will happen to her, mistakes made, regrets, life. The other, thinking about all of the loss she experienced in her 17 years: about being alone again, about losing another mother, about seeing her mother's eyes close in death. She also began to feel confused about the direction that her life would take on next.

That night, while battling her regular nightly demons, she now had a new one to fight: the new sense that she would soon be alone in the world. In her room, she sat thinking about God and all that she had learned while in church, and from Ms. Strickland. She thought about the Bible; the seventh book of Ecclesiastes, the fourteenth verse that is written, *When times are good, be happy; but when times are bad, consider: God has made the one as well as the other...* Then she thought about Deuteronomy 31:6, *Be strong and courageous. Do not be afraid or terrified because of them, for the Lord your God goes with you; he will never leave you nor forsake you.* She could not get the two verses out of her mind. She felt confused - how could God allow such terrible things to happen to her? What had she done to deserve the amount of pain she had experienced and would experience in her short life? If God was responsible for her troubles, then why serve Him? If He will never forsake you, then why, after so many years, can't she forget? Why does she still smell her attackers? Why does she still hurt? For the first time, she began to feel anger; and before the night ended, that anger turned to rage.

CHAPTER 8

Weeks after the ruckus at the Langston estate, things seemed to return to normal. Anna served her suspension and pleaded for her father's forgiveness. She wrote letters of apology to both Principal Mackenzie and the McFadden family for her behavior, and she expressed her regret about her terrible actions. Joan continued her life as the model wife to her husband; she continued to host lavish parties, playing hostess to guests and catering to her husband's every whim. However, there was one fundamental change in the Langston household; instead of one Langston not sleeping at home at night, there were two. Anna now decided that with her father barely returning home, she didn't run the risk of getting caught by sneaking out. She figured that she could get away with staying a few nights with her boyfriend Jonathan, so long as she returned before the morning.

"I can't believe how good it feels to be laying in your arms like this," Anna smiled as she nestled her head onto Jonathan's bare chest.

"Trust me Ma, I can get used to this."

"I wish I didn't have to leave so early in the morning, but it won't be for too much longer. The school year will be over before you know it, and then I'll be out of my house - then we can really make it happen."

"You know you always have a place right here with me."

"That's why I love you."

"And you know I couldn't love you more."

She drifted off to sleep, completely relaxed knowing that she was cradled in the loving arms of the man that she was destined to spend the rest of her life with. While she lay sleeping, and while Jonathan held the woman he loved in his arms, they were interrupted by the vibration of his cellular phone. He gazed at the clock on the nightstand which read 3:26. His heart began to race. He slowly shifted his body to release Anna from the comfort of their position and sat up to check the text message.

I hope you didn't think that one payment was going to silence me forever. We all know that with men the flesh is weak, and you are definitely a weak man. It must be hard to be a grown-ass man in love with a bitch still in high school, living under her daddy's thumb. Hey, that's none of my business. I don't think your pretty little girlfriend would like to hear the details of how you put all that equipment to good use on me. How you licked and sucked on my pussy or how you fucked me all over that king sized bed of yours. I have a vivid recollection, and wouldn't mind recounting every sordid detail to her. You know what I want, and how I want it. Don't be late.

Jonathan's mind began to race, and the memory of that day began to flood back to him. He was leaving work, thinking about a gift he wanted to buy for Anna. It had been almost a week since he last saw her. He understood that she was busy with her studies and the extracurricular activities that she was forced to participate in. Whenever she could call him from a pay phone or send him e-mails, she would. He longed for more interaction; but he was patient. He loved her. They shared a connection that he couldn't explain, but the connection was so real that it didn't warrant one. He decided to stop at a local bar for happy hour; he wanted to unwind before searching the mall for the perfect gift to place a smile on the face of the woman he loved. Having finished his second drink, he noticed one of the most strikingly beautiful women he'd ever seen making her way towards him. He hoped she wouldn't find her way to sit next to him. He had consumed his first two drinks way too quickly and he began to feel a slight buzz. He also wanted to remain focused on "feeling good", and later, focus on getting something nice for Anna.

Indeed, this woman sat down right next to him. Her scent went straight into his nostrils - it intoxicated him. He tried not to stare at her, but her eyes drew him in. Before he knew it, he spoke. "Damn, Mama, you have some beautiful eyes!"

"So, I've been told."

"So, you're one of those?"

"One of what?"

"One of those women who can't say 'thank you'."

"I'll say 'thank you' when you offer to buy me a drink."

"What will you have?"

"A slow screw against the wall."

"We're still talking about the drink, right?" he said with a chuckle.

"Yes. Now if you're really good to me you'll learn that I don't like anything slow," she replied, licking her lips.

He swallowed hard, and then took a quick gulp of his drink. Feeling his manhood rise, he knew he was in for trouble. "What's your name? I'm Jonathan," he offered, at a loss for words.

"Sapphire."

"It's a pleasure, Mama."

"I'm sure the pleasure will be all yours." Overtly flirting at this point, she let her intentions be known.

"I... I... I have a girlfriend."

"I'm not trying to be your wife, daddy; I'm just trying to get to know you better. Can I get to know you?" She paused, "By the way, where is your girlfriend now?"

"She's home."

"Whose home?"

"Her home."

"Then we have time for a few more drinks, don't we?"

"I should be going, Ma."

"If you insist," she replied. As he made an attempt to get up, she leaned over and kissed him. Sapphire knew that men could hardly resist her. She kissed him slowly, her soft lips caressing his, her delicate hands gently placed on the side of his face. He became lost in the moment. She stood up and pulled him in for yet another kiss; this time she gently massaged the outline of his erect manhood and whispered in his ear, "Let me have you just once, Daddy. Please... I want to feel you inside me."   Even though he tried to resist her advances, he couldn't.

At his house, Jonathan took Sapphire into his arms and kissed her. He knew what he was doing was wrong, but the flesh is weak indeed. The specimen in front of him possessed the beauty that men would kill to be able to have in their possession. He undressed her slowly, taking in her beauty. He pleaded with her to pleasure herself as he watched. She obliged his pleas. Jonathan began to massage his manhood as she released moans that played like music to his ears. He decided to aid his companion by way of delivering oral stimulation to her nether regions. She massaged and licked her breast while he performed the task that seemed to please both of them equally. Because Sapphire is not one to relinquish all of her control, she told him that she wanted to taste his thick manhood. She performed fellatio as if it were an art form studied at the best universities. Jonathan's body quivered and shook; he never experienced a woman who could tackle the size of his package without surrendering to the human gag reflex. She purposely brought him to the point where he wanted to orgasm, and then she would stop. She'd tease him, keeping him under her control. Jonathan was lost in a state of bliss.

Sapphire then mounted Jonathan and rubbed herself against him. She allowed her juices to drip on him. She whispered in his ear, "You want to fuck this, don't you Daddy?"

"Yes Mama!" he screamed without hesitation. He momentarily thought of Anna, but still pushed her to the back of his mind. The flesh felt too good at that moment. He reached over and grabbed a single condom from the drawer of his nightstand. Soon after the golden wrapper hit the floor, the sounds of two adult bodies intermixed in a raw, animalistic passion filled the room. Skin against skin - panting, smacking, moaning, licking, sucking, then the finish; Jonathan reached his peak. She allowed Jonathan to bask in the glow of experiencing her gem.

"Did you like that, Daddy?"

"Ay, Dios mío Mama...Yes!"

As she got up and began to dress, she asked him, "Do you fuck Anna the way you just fucked me?"

Startled, he looks at Sapphire. "What did you say?"

"You heard me... I'm talking about Anna, you know? Your girlfriend?"

"I never told you her name."

"Jonathan, look, let's not play games. I know everything about you. I know you've been sneaking around with that young girl for more than a year. I know that you're a Mortgage Broker, and quite a successful one at that. You've brokered the mortgage for that new casino that's going to be built upstate, didn't you?"

"How the fuck -"

"I have my ways, Mr. Torres, and my silence can be bought for the right price. You know little Anna would be just devastated to know how my legs were just wrapped around your powerful shoulders." The tone in her voice illustrated her seriousness. He sat there, not knowing what to say or to do. He knew he made a monumental mistake in giving in to temptation; he also knew he didn't want to lose or hurt Anna. He loved her. He was so confused. How did she know so much about him? Why was she doing this? What did she really want?

"Why are you doing this to me?"

"You are a means to an end, Jonathan. My silence is as golden as the Magnum wrapper lying on the floor. I want money, and you have plenty of it. You pay me - I stay silent. That will be our arrangement. The details of everything else are not important. You give me your number; I will text you with instructions, you will follow them. It's that simple."

"And you'll leave me alone?"

"You got it!"

"Fine... Now get the fuck out."

"Watch the way you speak to me - I'd hate to get angry and forget that you're a nice guy," she snapped as she walked over to his pants that laid crumpled on the floor. She picked them up and retrieved his wallet, took out a business card and the cash she found inside, then exited the room leaving Jonathan there, shaken. Jonathan was left in bed with a hodgepodge of feelings that spanned the gamut: from guilt, anger, and shame, to confusion, sorrow, and fear.

Jonathan placed the cell phone back on his dresser and looked at Anna. He knew he would have to deliver a check in the morning. How long would this black cloud follow him before it became so saturated that rain must fall? How long could he fall victim to the demands of one person with no heart? He longed to turn back the hands of time and forever erase the mistake of that one night, but he knew he couldn't. For now, he would pay for her silence, but for how long?

CHAPTER 9

For most of Joan's adult life, one could have described her as desperate; she was the clichéd desperate housewife. She longed for attention, but didn't receive it. She tried her best to be perfect, but failed miserably. She lived for everyone else, but never herself. Her quest to make others happy ultimately contributed to wasted years on a man who failed to show her a shred of human decency. After hearing her husband's callous words a few weeks ago, a part of her died; a part of the life that she had long fought to hold on to had died. She finally accepted the notion that her marriage was over. It's difficult for a woman to truly come to grips with the idea that the one they pledged themselves to, mind, body, and soul before God, family, and friends wouldn't be there for a lifetime.

Joan sat gazing at her wedding ring. "Jason, life sometimes plays cruel jokes. Look at the circular band around my finger.

It's supposed to signify a love that is supposed to last for eternity. I don't even know when he stopped loving me. This ring is a lie. That estate is a lie. The only truth I have is Anna."

"Girl, you have more than that. You have to stop looking at all the negatives you have going on in your life and begin to look at what's right. You do live in a home most people would kill for. You are an educated Black... umm whatever you are. Mutt..." he said with a chuckle. "You are fierce. You can give any twenty- or thirty-something heffa a run for her money. Need I repeat myself? Honey, you are fierce! Plus, you know your way around the kitchen, so don't let that no-good-ass-man ruin you or define you."

"I just don't know what I'm gonna do, J. Part of me will always love him. I think things would have been different if I could have given him more children."

"There you go, making excuses. Girl, cut that shit out. That was over 15 years ago. If he wanted more children that badly, he would have been more than happy to adopt when you brought it up the hundred times you did. His sorry ass used that against you for far too long and I won't sit here and listen to you beat yourself up about it anymore. God allows certain things to happen for a reason. He blessed you with Anna, and from what I can see, she is as close to perfect as a child can get. Count that blessing."

"I know, but I can't get the years of torment out my head. I've felt so low for so long."

"Bitch, do you want me to go cut him? You know I will! Let me go get a scalpel from Chris! *How you doing?* "

"As tempting as that sounds, I have to find a way to deal with the years of shit that has built up in my head on my own. But there is something I haven't told you. You just have to promise not to go crazy."

Jason looks at her oddly then begins to chant, "Namu-myoho-renge-kyo, Namu-myoho-renge-kyo, Namu-myoho-renge-kyo. O.K. I'm calm and I promise not to go crazy... I saw *What's Love Got to Do with It*, and I read Tina Turner's book like 3 times. What's so bad that I have to keep calm?"

"It's not so much what I have to tell you, but what I have to show you. I've gotten two different envelopes over the past two months, and both envelopes didn't have a return address. The last one I got I received the day after Greg and I had our last fight."

"What was in the envelopes?"

Joan reached down into her crocodile Hermes handbag, pulled out two envelopes, and handed them to Jason. Her eyes began to water, then the tears began to flow. She couldn't control her body from shaking from thinking about the contents of the envelopes. Jason, looking at his best friend, knew that now was not the time for him to joke. He opened the first envelope and a rush of heat crept up his spine and traveled to the back of his neck. He then opened the next envelope. The sight of what was in the envelopes caused him to drop the contents to the floor. He gasped. "What the fuck is this? Is this some kind of joke?"

"I don't think it is."

"Then we need to get to the bottom of it. We need some answers. I'll utilize all my resources; and I'll get Chris's help. Girl, we'll turn Heaven and Hell until we unearth this shit. Joan, no matter what, I got your back. Know this!"

Joan didn't think things could be any worse, but should her suspicions be confirmed by the investigation, then she would breathe life to the adage, *hell hath no fury like a woman scorned...*

CHAPTER 10

Anger, rage, confliction, and suppression of one's feelings are all the ingredients necessary for a cocktail of volatility. In Sapphire's young life, she not only drank this elixir, but she also let it permeate every fiber of her being. During her senior year of high school, when she should have been jubilantly planning for the prom and graduation, she was finalizing her legal emancipation, making funeral arrangements, and becoming well-acquainted with the staff at the local Hospice facility.

Hospice care is designed to aid the terminally ill in order to ensure comfort during the final days of life. Doctors, nurses, social workers, counselors, and therapists all work in conjunction to assure that the patient has both quality care and dignity when passing on from this life. Ms. Strickland's condition deteriorated rather quickly, soon after she delivered the news to Sapphire. Sapphire internalized her pain, as was customary for her, and wore the mask of the 'good daughter' to Ms. Strickland. She'd attend school regularly and spend her evenings by Ms. Strickland's side. She was tireless in ensuring that Ms. Strickland was receiving the best care. There were several nights when Sapphire would sit and watch the woman she looked to as her mother breathe shallowly. She'd watch and pray in earnest that a miracle would happen and her condition would improve, but she knew that would not happen. She wanted to bring her one last piece of joy before her eyes closed for eternal rest; she wanted to see that glow in her eyes, even though they were now weak. She knew time was working against her.

The following morning, Sapphire walked into her guidance counselor's office. In great detail, she explained to him about Ms. Strickland and why her usually phenomenal grades had taken such a sharp decline. She noted to him that she'd be willing to do anything to show Ms. Strickland just one last report card that would make her proud before she passed away. Noticing the desperation in her eyes, he decided to take full advantage of the situation. "I'm sorry Sapphire, but your grades this last marking period were not on par with the standard you set your previous years here. However, I can talk to your teachers and see if they'd be willing to give you some extra time to make up the work you've missed."

"But I don't have that kind of time," she wailed, beginning to cry. "I know this is a lot to ask, but is there a way we can just print a report card with straight A's? I just want to make her proud, even if it's a lie... please Mr. Young."

"Not only is that out of the question, but I have a moral and ethical responsibility not to falsify documents. You're asking a lot, Miss Taylor."

"Please. I don't know what else to do. She could be dead right now for all I know. Please help me. She has saved me in more ways than you'll ever know. I owe her my life. Please. Don't say no... I'll do anything - I'll stay after school, I'll clean your office, I'll do extra work... I need to do this. I won't tell anyone a thing!"

Sapphire fell to her knees and wept. She covered her face and sobbed. She thought of losing her savior. In that moment, she could not think of her demons, her studies, her applications for college, nothing. All Sapphire could think of was placing one last smile on the face of her angel, one last time.

"I hate to see such a beautiful young woman cry like this," Mr. Young sighed, printing a copy of a report card from the printer. Walking over to the crying mass on the floor, he adds, "While I'm doing such an important favor for you, you're going to have to do something for me in return that I trust will stay strictly between us - or Ms. Strickland will never smile again."

Sapphire looked at him, flabbergasted. He dropped the report card on the floor and slowly combed her hair with his hands. He then brushed the hair that covered her left eye away from her face. She shook and turned numb; she wanted to scream, wanted to fight. She thought about God, got mad, felt rage, and thought of Ms. Strickland, but finally, she gave in...

On the way to the hospital, Sapphire rationalized her actions as best as she could. She allowed what happened to happen for a purpose larger than herself. Upon arrival to the hospital, she was greeted by Dr. Lee and a social worker. They asked Sapphire to follow them into an office. Sapphire's instincts told her something was wrong, but no amount of preparation could have prepared her for the blow she received.

"We've been trying to reach you for the past two hours. I'm sorry to have to tell you this, but Marie passed away while sleeping. She's at peace now."

The doctor and social worker continued to talk, but she heard nothing. She saw their lips and hands moving, but no sound. When it seemed that they were finished talking to her, she asked, "Where is she? I'd like to see her."

"Of course," the doctor motioned towards the door.

As Sapphire stood gazing at the lifeless body of her mother, she shed no tears. She was done shedding tears. She loved this woman and had allowed a man to defile her body in order to place a smile on her face; she never even got the chance to say goodbye. It was his fault. It was God's fault. It was the fault of men. God gave her the looks that made men salivate, and what did she ever get out of it? Rape, a life of pain, robbed of saying goodbye to the woman she loved most in life. She knew that now that she had no one to live for but herself. She was going to live life her way or no way at all. God endowed her with one gift, and that gift was looks; she'd use it to get what she wanted. From this moment forward, she vowed that those who crossed her path had better watch out.

As Sapphire arrived home, she placed calls to the funeral home and to the pastor to arrange for the burial. She knew that Ms. Strickland wasn't fond of the showiness of funerals. She also placed a call to the school. It was customary for guidance counselors to remain in school late to work with students and parents on the college application process. She pretended to be Mrs. Young, and told the school secretary that it was an emergency.

"Dear, what's wrong?" Mr. Young answered in a concerned tone.

"This is Sapphire," she answered coldly.

"Oh, Miss Taylor, I was told that this call was from my wife," he said nervously.

"My mother died," Saphire replied with no emotion.

"I'm sorry to hear that. Would you like for me to inform the secretaries in the office that you will not be in for a few days?"

"I'm calling to tell you that while you were committing a felony, my mother died without me. I'm calling because I'm telling you that the straight A's will stay right where they are... you know, the ones you falsified. I'm calling to tell you that from now on if you like your freedom, you'll do exactly what I say, when I say it."

"Miss Taylor, I will not be threat-"

Click

CHAPTER 11

After lecturing all day and enduring a long and exhausting night of listening to his wife suggest that they try counseling to help salvage their marriage, all Professor Langston could do was think about becoming lost in the scent of the alluring Sapphire. He knew in his heart that he had not been the best father, nor had he been the best husband; he wasn't even close. He was overbearing and cold, and in the past, he had the occasional extra-marital affair. With Sapphire, however, it was different. Prior to meeting her, he'd have his way with students who'd clearly found him attractive. He found it sexually arousing to venture over the boundary line of the student-teacher dynamic, which is most certainly taboo. He'd happily oblige the young co-eds that were willing, pacifying their curiosity.

If you were to ask him if he loved his wife and daughter he would unequivocally say yes, because he did. However, he always longed for more. He was a man that wanted more, and he strived for perfection. If he saw something as flawed, he'd detach himself from it. Sapphire was the perfect gem to him. She wasn't one of the students who threw themselves at him; she showed him tenderness and she made love passionately. She never asked for him to give her favorable grades, but she thanked him when he did. She never nagged him; instead she listened intently to his problems. She was understanding and showed genuine interest in Gregory, not Professor Langston. She was an escape from having to live the life he felt compelled to live. She also captivated his senses. She drew him in every time he saw her… her hair, her eyes, her smell, her taste, her touch. He knew he was in trouble when he felt his heart splintering between his life at home and the woman who became the gem of his world.

The Professor reminded his students, "Don't forget that your exam starts promptly at 5:00 next week." Because this was his last class of the day, he eagerly made his departure toward his office. All he could think about was calling Sapphire. He needed to hear her voice. He was supposed to be meeting Joan for dinner, but he figured she could wait until he finished talking to Sapphire. When he arrived to his office, he opened the door to a surprise.

Sapphire, standing at his file cabinet, quickly turned around. "I thought you would never get here. Hey baby," she smiled.

"What are you doing in here? I was just about to call you."

"I'm waiting on you silly. I wanted to surprise you; I guess I was successful."

"Yes, you are, but I don't like for people to be in my office unattended. How did you get in here?"

"I'm quite resourceful," she purred while walking over to kiss him. "I've been waiting to do that *all* day. But if you want me to leave..." she paused while looking into his eyes, "I will."

"No, no. Baby, don't go anywhere."

While kissing his neck, she starts to unbuckle his belt. He lets out a soft moan, reaching for his phone.

"What are you doing?"

"Let me call my wife and tell her I'm going to be a little late."

"A little?"

"Fuck it!" The professor grinned, dropping his phone.

The two lovers experienced each other's bodies until the Professor stretched himself out on the floor, exhausted. He didn't want the experience to end. He wanted to lie on her supple breasts for forever and a day. She snuggled next to him, thinking about what she discovered prior to the professor walking into his office. *"This asshole!"* she thought to herself. *"All men are the same - and this one will pay worst of all -, but not until I get exactly what I want out of the deal."*

Breaking the silence between the two, she whispers, "Baby, I'm going to have to get going. I forgot that I have a few things that I have to get done before class in the morning."

"Are you sure you have to leave? I don't feel like going home to deal with that bitch right now. Can't you just stay or can't I come home with you tonight?"

"Go home to your wife, but tomorrow we can meet again if you'd like." She knew very well that he would be unable to meet her from what she read in his files.

"Tomorrow will be no good. I… umm… I have this thing with my daughter that I have to take care of so I'll be pretty occupied."

"Okay. Well, just call me. You know you can have me any time you want me," she smiled with a wink. She then planted soft kiss on his lips as she got up from the floor where they both were laying. While she dressed he watched her, studying her body. He smiled as she put on her clothes more slowly than usual, knowing that he was enjoying the view.

The following day, Professor Langston drove down Lexington Boulevard, better known as the financial district, in a car that wasn't his own. He was taking pictures of a young beauty and an extremely handsome Hispanic gentleman walking hand in hand into Kevin's Coffee. After a few minutes, they walked to a posh new restaurant, The Willow. When the couple exited the restaurant, they walked to a white Jaguar where he opened her door for her, but before she got in the car, they embraced for a rather long kiss. Professor Langston snapped away at the public display of affection, and then slammed down the camera. He watched the Hispanic gentleman then run into one of the large high-rise buildings that housed one of the largest mortgage brokerage firms in the state. Moments later, the gentleman returned and the couple sped off, as did Professor Langston. Unbeknownst to them all, Sapphire watched from afar. The information she gained proved to be more valuable than she could have ever imagined because it could help to ruin Professor Langston and bring her the payday she felt she so richly deserved.

CHAPTER 12

Love can be a beautiful thing when two people share it equally, however, it can prove to be quite dangerous when one of those people feels the sting of rejection. Such was the case of Saara Conroy, Professor Langston's personal secretary and assistant of eight years. Saara began her tenure working under Professor Langston as a temp, and soon after her husband ended their marriage of more than twelve years. She was told that she loved him 'too much' and that her love 'smothered him'. Saara was left to raise their two children alone. As most women know, when men leave the picture, child support and limited state assistance prove not to be sufficient. As a result, Saara sought work through a temp agency. Ultimately, she was assigned a temp-to-hire position at the University working for one the most respected professors, Professor Langston. She hoped that her hard work would secure her a permanent position. At the conclusion of her first meeting with Professor Langston, she knew there was something special about him. She was drawn to him, his cologne, and the way his pants fit snugly around his rear and accentuated what he offered in the front. She found his intelligence, and most importantly, the respect he commanded, two of his most attractive features. Saara knew instinctually that she would love to work for this man and that she had to secure the position, no matter the cost.

Saara set out to learn everything she could about Professor Langston. The first thing she did was to learn whether he preferred coffee or tea, and how he liked it. She came to work respectfully dressed and made sure that his needs were always met, no matter how tedious the task. She never mentioned that she had children, nor did she place any pictures of her children on her desk; she'd heard too many stories of women who use their children as excuses not to go in to work and didn't want her children to serve as a handicap. Whenever he'd ask her to stay late, she'd oblige and excuse herself to make the arrangements for childcare in private. She wanted to ensure that she proved, without question, that she was dedicated to the job. Within two months' time, Professor Langston called her into his office. "Ms. Conroy, may I see you for a moment?"

"Yes sir?"

"I wanted to let you know that you've been doing an amazing job since you've started."

"Thank you so much."

"I've been through several assistants and none of them have been able to maintain the level of professionalism that you've demonstrated since you've been here and its only been two months."

"I'm just grateful to have been given the opportunity to work under you. You're so well-respected."

"No need to flatter me, I'm lucky to have you. This brings me to my next question. We need to change your status around here. I'm ready to make you an offer, but I need you to understand what this job truly entails first."

"There's more?"

"This job comes with the added responsibility of maintaining the confidentiality of not only the students, but also my confidentiality as well."

She paused, trying to completely understand the meaning of what he was saying. "Yes sir, I'm prepared to do that."

"I need to feel confident that I can trust you in all things; like if I'm here late and my wife should call, you would respect my privacy."

"It wouldn't be my place to say anything, Sir."

"So if I told you to relay a specific message, you would do as you were told?"

"It would be my job..."

"That's what I wanted to hear. So, my final question is, would you like to accept a permanent position as my personal assistant and secretary?"

"A hundred times, yes!"

"Then welcome aboard. I'll have the university contracts ready for you in the morning."

"Thank you so much! You won't regret this; I promise."

"I'm sure I won't. Now go and celebrate. I'll see you bright and early in the morning."

Saara felt on top of the world when she accomplished what she set out to do. She was making a way for her and her children. She no longer depended on a man who viewed her as being 'too much'. She secured a way to provide, and she did so in a respectable way. She did, however, have a few reservations. She didn't like the provision that she would have to lie to his wife should he tell her to. She also did not like the fact that such a respectable man admitted, in such a vague way and without any sense of remorse that he cheats on his wife. What kind of man would do such a thing? *Who really is the man that I've been working with for the past two months?* she pondered. She saw a man of power, position, and intelligence. *There must be something wrong at home,* she rationalized. *He must love his wife and child so much that he simply didn't want to hurt them. Why else would a man who has so much power and prestige need to cheat? If he feels the need, then she must be a terrible wife.*

For now, Saara would take the command from her new boss to celebrate her new job. First, she would call her ex-husband and gloat over her new position. She'd tell him that his leaving was now his loss and that you could never love someone 'too much'. She'd then go home and take her children to a late dinner, have a glass of wine, and think about her new job and the life to come. The future, she thought, was much like traveling on an open highway: you'd rather do it with a companion than alone. Could the professor one day be that companion? What about his admission to infidelity? She knew in time that all her questions would be answered; she just needed to be patient and coast down the highway alone for now...

CHAPTER 13

For Saara Conroy, working for Professor Langston proved to be harder than she ever imagined. She learned, quite early in her tenure, how truly demanding the Professor could be. He demanded strict adherence to his word, and any deviation from it came with serious consequences. Saara was once scolded, as if she were a child, when she returned to the office ten minutes early. He was having a 'private meeting' with a student which required that no one, not even she, be around. She knew all too well what transpired between Professor Langston and the student. On another occasion, Mrs. Langston pushed her way past Saara to enter the Professor's office. Mrs. Langston wanted to wait for him while he finished teaching a class. Saara tried her best to warn Professor Langston before his return, thinking that he would be pleased that she cautioned him well in advance. Instead, he informed Saara that he needed to meet with a student in private and then was told to excuse herself. She then tried reiterating her warning more forcefully, however, he laughed at her and told her to stop joking around. When he returned to his office, the argument that ensued between Joan and her husband did not bode well for Saara. Saara was ultimately reprimanded for 'allowing' Joan into his office, which caused him to cancel the 'meeting' with his student.

Even with the demands of the job, Saara still loved working for Professor Langston. She still found herself intrigued by him; his power still drew her in. The more she saw Joan, the more she detested her. Every time Joan was in her presence, she seemed to be nagging or upsetting her boss; which in turn made him take his anger out on those who were his subordinates. There were days when he looked as if he barely slept. She blamed Joan and thought; *I bet she started with him again. He needs a _real_ woman.* Saara never felt jealous of the girls that she knew he was violating his marriage vows with, but rather, she excused it. In her mind, a woman should complement her husband and cherish him, love him totally, and do as he says. Joan didn't strike her as that type. *No wonder she drove him into the beds of other women*, she smirked.

After working for the Professor for eight years, Saara decided that she could no longer bear to simply look at him from the sidelines. Over the years, she was able to learn the Professor's routines as well as his likes and dislikes. She also felt that she was better suited for him than the wife he already had. All she needed was for him to afford her the opportunity that she felt that she earned: making him happy personally, because she was already pleasing him professionally.

Saara closed the notebook that she wrote in on a daily basis and placed it in her pocketbook. She then knocked on the Professor's office door. "Come in."

"I know you're grading papers, but I thought you could use a drink." She brought him his favorite drink: imported vodka with a splash of cranberry juice.

"That's exactly what I need. You know me so well!" he grinned, sipping his drink. "Damn," he swallowed, "that's good." He motioned for her to sit at one of the armchairs in front of his desk. "Have one with me; you've been working all day."

"Thanks, I will. You know It's been just over eight years now; can you believe it?"

"Has it been that long?"

"Yes, and I told you that you wouldn't regret it."

"What can I say? You were right," he admitted, turning around to place a file in his cabinet. She took advantage of the opportunity by unbuttoning the buttons on her blouse to expose her cleavage.

"You've been looking so tense lately. I know it's none of my business, but is everything okay with you and Joan?"

Still facing the file cabinet, he replied, "Same shit." He closed the drawer, then sat down looking tense. "Sometimes I just don't want to go home. Sometimes I just don't know what to do."

"I'm so sorry to hear that. I wish I could help you."

"Pour me another drink, would ya?"

"Anything..."

"Recently I have seen light at the end of this dark tunnel."

"Really?"

Looking directly at Saara, he continued, "Yes. I've felt more like a man recently - more than I have in years. I mean, it's the way I've been taken care of... It's what's been done for me… It's what we share when it's just the two of us that has me questioning everything I have at home."

He closed his eyes and reclined in his chair. She walked over to him and began to massage his shoulders. His body submitted to the sensation her hands created as they manipulated his tension away. Before long, he felt her tongue massage the side of his neck, which caused him to jump out of his chair. "Saara! What are you doing?"

"What do you mean? I'm making you feel good," she smiled seductively.

"You clearly have the wrong idea."

"Gregory, I don't have the wrong idea. We've shared so much over the past eight years and it's time you give up those young girls and allow a *real* woman to take care of you."

"What makes you think you're that woman?"

"It's because of what we share. Gregory, I know you. I know you better than any woman on this earth. I know that your wife drove you to do the things you do, but I don't care about those things; I don't even fault you for it. I love you, and I've loved you for years."

"I *don't* love you," he sighed with growing frustration.

"You just told me that you're questioning your marriage. You're seeing light at the end of the tunnel. You just looked me in my eyes and said it to me." Her disappointment and desperation increased with each sentence she spoke.

"I wasn't talking about you, I was talking about Sapphire Taylor!" he yelled with an extreme amount of irritation.

"Sapphire Taylor?" she repeated in disbelief.

"Get the hell out of my office! Your conduct is beneath one who expects to maintain employment with me," he hissed, unable to contain his irritation any longer.

"What are you saying?" Her voice quivered with hurt and rejection.

"Tomorrow you should be looking for another job. I'll write you a letter of recommendation, but I can no longer have you here."

"But..."

"This is not up for discussion; button your blouse. Try having a little tact!"

Saara's face became stoic. She turned and exited his office, grabbed her bag from her desk, and left. While driving home, tears ran down her face. She heard the words from her former husband echo in her mind, *You're too fucking much...you're psycho!* Was he right? How could she explain getting let go from the job she maintained for the past eight years? How could she face the world? How could she live, knowing that people would judge her? Her ex-husband was right. Damn him for being right! Why did she fall for the Professor?

When she got home, she went into the bathroom and poured her favorite vanilla bath crystals into the running water. She then lit candles, took her book out of her purse, stripped, and got in the tub. She began to write about her day and all that had transpired. She was especially sure to write about how she professed her love for Professor Langston which was rebuffed; how he informed her of his feelings for the beautiful, blue-eyed Sapphire Taylor. the student she recounted numerous times in her diary. Saara noted the following:

> *I once thought of life as a highway that you either travel alone or with a companion. I never thought I would be one of those destined to travel it alone. My children are gone now - making*

their way. He took the one thing from me I had left and crushed my heart in the process. I did everything I could for this man and he treated me like my ex-husband Thomas did. Why is it wrong to love? Why do people force me to leave when I show them love? Gregory's infatuation with Sapphire Taylor made him do this. He would have loved me if she didn't come between us. She cast a spell on him. In eight years, I've never seen him act like this about any of the other women he's slept with. How could I possibly compete? I choose not to take this highway ride alone. A life without love is not a life worth living.

The following day, Professor Langston tried to call Saara but there was no answer. As a result, he called the same temp agency where he found her and secured a replacement. Shortly thereafter, everything returned to business as usual on campus.

The following week, as Anna lay in Jonathan's arms watching the news, a reporter interviewed a landlord describing how he found a tenant dead in her tub. "Yeah, the smell coming from the apartment was awful, so I had to go in. When I went in there she was laying in the tub with an empty pill bottle right next to her."

The Asian news correspondent ended the segment, informing viewers that she would follow up her report with comments from the victim's daughter at 11:00. When the name of the victim flashed across the screen, Anna sat up. *Saara Conroy found dead, details at 11.*

CHAPTER 14

In Ms. Strickland's will, she bequeathed to Sapphire a small sum of money to be used for her college education. This wasn't at all a surprise to Sapphire when she heard the news at the reading of Ms. Strickland's will; however, what was a surprise was finding out that Ms. Strickland had a son whom Sapphire never met, nor was she ever told about. He was mentioned during the reading of the will, but he was not present due to his incarceration for a drug-related murder. Ms. Strickland's last gesture of love warmed Sapphire's heart. However, she knew that with the grants, financial aid, and scholarships she obtained due to her hard work, the cost of her education would be of no consequence to her. She also knew that she could now count on the financial backing of a particular guidance counselor to ensure that should she need anything along the way, she'd have it.

Graduation for Sapphire proved to be bittersweet; she accomplished what many in her circumstance would not have been able to, but the one she loved most was not there to witness it. When her name was called during the ceremony, she arose and crossed the stage just as her peers did. She looked out at a sea of people...none there for her. She became transfixed on a particular figure that was walking down the aisle towards the stage. Sapphire wiped her eyes, proceeded to exit the stage, and took her seat. When the ceremony ended and the graduates tossed their caps in the air, Sapphire just sat in her seat, motionless, caps pelting her. Her mind was completely adrift. The image of the person she saw in the sea of faces as she stood on the stage was familiar, yet strange. The image had an effect on her and she didn't know why. The principal announced that the graduates were to proceed to the reception area of the arena where they were to say their final goodbyes to their teachers and peers. Sapphire decided that she would decline the opportunity to do so because she just wanted to leave and begin the next chapter of her life; what better way to start than to visit Ms. Strickland's gravesite?

While driving to her destination, she felt a sense of emptiness. She needed a release; she needed to feel the comfort of Ms. Strickland's arms outstretched and holding her. She knew in Ms. Strickland's arms that all the terrible things in the world ceased to exist. She provided balance to the craziness of Sapphire's life; she was the anchor to her ship. She knew that once she reached Ms. Strickland's final resting place that she would unburden her soul and tell Ms. Strickland all of the things she always wanted to tell her when she was alive.

Once Sapphire reached the burial site, she laid a dozen roses upon Ms. Strickland's grave, took off her graduation gown, and laid it upon the ground as if it were a blanket.

"Mommy, I did it. I finished just like I know you would have wanted me to. I finished with an A average too. I'm sure you're proud of me." Sapphire's expression changed and then her eyes began to fill with tears. "There is so much I want to tell you, so much that I wish you were here to help me with. I haven't always been honest with you. For so long I've pretended to be happy. I still relive the night before I came to live with you. Mommy, it still haunts me; it never leaves me." The more she spoke, the more her words became broken because of her crying and her attempts to regain composure.

Sapphire lived in the moment; she was releasing her inner demons in hopes that her mother would hear her; that her mother would send her a sign that things would magically improve. "Mommy, I'm so sorry I wasn't there for you when you passed. I wanted to be there so badly. I tried so hard to be there. I tried...I tried...I *tried*. I just couldn't get there in time. I did something I wish I could take back. I did something so terrible. Mommy, I can't even say it. It was horrible, and it hurt so badly. I just wanted to see you and hold your hand. I was denied that right; he denied me. Mommy, I'm so sorry. Please forgive me....please, Mommy."

Sapphire's cathartic expression to her mother was interrupted by a voice that caused her heart to nearly stop. The voice caused confusion, surprise, and then rage to surface before Sapphire could turn around to face the source of the interruption...

"Baby, Mommy's here..."

CHAPTER 15

Investigating an unfaithful spouse's actions can be a daunting task when the initial information one has to work with is extremely ambiguous. Joan and her trusted friend Jason were up for the challenge to discover who sent her the envelopes and what their contents actually meant. Joan resolved in her mind that her marriage was over, but she needed a few questions answered and she needed the truth; not the truth as Gregory saw it. While the friends sat at their favorite spa getting their weekly manicures and pedicures, they started to devise a plan.

"J, when I got the first envelope, I seriously thought it was a joke. I mean, we know Greg cheats but I always felt he had better judgment. I know I deserve much better, I shouldn't be disrespected, and I put up with more than I should. But damn!

Is he that stupid to be putting my life in danger by not using protection?"

"Girl, you know men only think with one head when those nasty bitches be throwing their twats around."

"But you know how he feels about protecting the Langston image."

"Yeah, you don't have to tell me. He hates the fact that you and I are even friends...Mr.-Fucking-Conservative! I still don't know why you married a fucking Republican," he quipped rolling his eyes and sucking his teeth.

"I just have to know if this bullshit is true."

"If it is, it has to be one of his students so let's start there."

"We definitely have to utilize Chris's help."

"Definitely..."

Once the two were finished with their manicures and pedicures, they decided to further their pampering session with deep-tissue massages. As they were both enjoying the pleasant fragrance of lavender, the tranquil sounds of water crashing against a seashore, and strong hands that felt as if they were sent from heaven, Joan's cell phone rang. "Hello?"

"Mom, it's me."

"Baby, is everything okay?"

"Yes...have you talked to Dad at all today?"

"No. At this very moment, your father is the last thing on my mind; I'm getting a massage."

"I'm sorry to interrupt, but I take it you didn't see the news last night?"

"No, I didn't baby, but can I call you in about 30 minutes?"

"Mommy, Saara killed herself!"

"What?"

"She killed herself; it was all over the news last night."

"I'll be home in an hour; meet me there."

"Okay. Love you."

"Love you too."

Joan lie there for a moment in silence. Why wouldn't her husband tell her that his secretary of eight years killed herself? Even though their marriage was in the horrible state that it was, that didn't seem to be something that Greg would fail to mention. She broke her silence and turned to Jason. "J?"

"Everything okay?"

"We gotta go! I'll fill you in on the way home; something is not right. We have to meet Anna."

CHAPTER 16

The unexpected death of a loved one can hit a person like a ton of bricks, especially when the loved one takes their own life. Many people view suicide as a selfish act, and more often than not, the victim's family is left with more questions than answers. In the case of Saara Conroy, her daughter Elise felt the typical emotions of a child whose parent who committed suicide. She had a host of questions, she felt the devastation of losing her mother; yet her mind couldn't escape the unknown. She questioned the circumstances that could bring her mother to such a place that she would have been driven to commit such an extreme act. Lost in her own sense of mourning, she couldn't bear to read through the pages of her mother's diary. The hunter green notebook that her mother prized and carried wherever she went held the answers to all of her questions - all she had to do was read its contents.

A print journalist knocked on her door while she was sitting in her living room gazing at a photo of her mother. "What?" she snapped, opening the door.

"I'm a journalist from DellSun News, and I was wondering if you'd be willing to answer a few questions about your mother?"

"Go straight to hell!" she yelled, slamming the door directly in his face.

As she sat back down, she looked at the photo again. She inadvertently placed it directly on the diary she took out of her mother's apartment. She opened the diary and began to read as the light of day began to fade. Her eyes watered as she learned about the treatment her mother suffered for loving her father 'too much', and that she felt that men disposed her. Other parts of the diary made her smile, especially when her mother would make mention of her deep love for her and her brother, and how she'd 'walk through hell' to make sure they'd have everything that they needed. Other parts of the diary made her sad and sick to her stomach to read: how she'd witnessed her boss's infidelity and was essentially forced to be a part of his deception. Elise firmly believed that there was no excuse for a man to cheat on a woman - no matter the circumstance. When she reached the final entry she, like many who deal with death, found a scapegoat to mitigate her pain. Professor Langston was the cause of her mother's death, and he needed to pay. He took her mother's life, and now she was going to take his. She was going to make him pray for death. .

CHAPTER 17

"What the fuck are you doing here?"

"I'm still your mother; don't talk to me like that!" she snapped in a knee-jerk reaction. After realizing her reaction, she brushed down her tattered hair, smiled, and continued, "I'm here to see my baby on her graduation day."

"I'm not your baby and you're not my mother. I buried my mother weeks ago."

"I know she took care of you for a while, but I'm better now. I was going through some thangs…I'm sorry baby-girl."

"Cut the shit, you fucking bitch. The nerve of you to come to me here!"

"You rushed off after the ceremony…I had to follow you."

"I wish it were you buried 6 feet under, you worthless druggie. Do you know what hell I've gone through? Do you know what hell I go through? You show up now when I'm practically a grown woman; why even come back into my life now? I don't need you nor want you in my life, you fucking crack-head."

"I'm off that shit, and I know I put you through a lot. But I'm still your mother and you can't change that. I deserve your respect and I want to make things right."

"How? How can you make things better, Dorris? Can you give me my virginity back? Can you give me the years of crying myself to sleep back? Can you give me the years of nightmares back? How about taking away my fear of men? Can you? Can you get the smell of those men out of my mind?"

"I know I could have done better as a mother, baby. But things could have been worse."

"*What*?!" Sapphire screeched. Before she knew it, she slapped the woman she now called Dorris on the cheek and then proceeded to wrap her hands around Dorris's throat, pushing her to the ground. "I fucking *hate* you. I fucking *hate* you...*bitch*." The years of repressed rage and anguish Sapphire carried with her were now unleashed upon Dorris. She never flinched at Dorris's attempts to abate her fury and she watched as the eyes of the woman she once called 'Mommy' now rolled to the back of her head. Without loosening her grip, she whispered in her ear, "So long as God grants you the ability to breathe, you'd be wise to stay the fuck away from me or I will kill you, bitch - you hear me? I will fucking *kill* you! My mother...my *real* mother...is dead. You're *nothing* to me." Sapphire rose to walk away, never looking back, leaving Dorris coughing on the ground.

CHAPTER 18

Why is it that the hardest circumstances one must overcome entail battling the very things that they are most insecure of? Joan and Jason sat sipping Mimosas the night after their meeting with Anna to talk about the contents of the envelopes and the progress, if any, they were making on obtaining information about the envelopes' contents. Joan, feeling defeated admitted, "J, I'm getting nowhere - I've tried everything I could think of and I've hit a dead end."

"I went to Chris, and he's been such a help. He said he was going to try to cross-reference the numbers off the bottom of what was in the second envelope and run it at the hospital, but it's going to be difficult because it's missing some key numbers."

"Well, the fact that he is even trying is a huge help. I don't know what I would do without you."

"Probably jump off a bridge," he answered with a laugh.

"What I really wish I could do is get into his office and get a master list of all of his students. But if he saw me coming, he'd know something was up."

"Too bad Saara killed herself. We could have picked her brain; she would have been ideal."

"No, that bitch didn't like me. I have an idea she wanted Greg herself."

"Why you say that?"

"Honey, I'm not stupid. You should see the way she would look at me when I'd come to the office. She'd give me that 'why-the-fuck-are-you-here?' look. You could cut the tension with a knife."

"She was another one of dem whores that needed a scalpel to the face, huh? Oh Lord, please forgive me! Let me stop speaking ill of the dead and desperate," Jason quipped as they both broke out in thunderous laughter.

"This is the most I've laughed in a long time. Truthfully, she could have had him if she wanted him that badly. I just don't give a shit - I just want the truth. No matter what, I just want the truth so I can have closure and move on with my life."

"Girl, I understand that, and you'll get it. You deserve peace of mind and that bastard deserves a swift kick in the ass. I still say you should let me cut him, and in the very least I say we jump him."

"He'll get what's coming to him; I can guarantee you that. Karma is a bitch!"

"So am I when it comes to my Joan and those who fuck with her!"

"J, trust me, Greg will get what is coming to him. We just need to stay focused on the task at hand and then we can deal with him. Every dog has his day."

They both replenished and raised their glasses to toast their renewed excitement to ensuring that the truth was found at all costs. Dr. Christopher Stevens was an invaluable aid to them, and they knew that finding a resource at the University would also be a benefit. They knew what they needed to do and exactly how they needed to do it. While she sipped her Mimosa, Joan scanned the two envelopes laying on the coffee table: one contained a pregnancy test that read positive and on top of the second was a duplicate copy of a sonogram with a note attached: *Professor Langston has been a naughty, naughty boy. I guess I'm giving him what you couldn't!*

CHAPTER 19

Professor Langston increasingly became bolder with flaunting his infidelity, and it became painfully evident by his frequent absences from home for nights at a time. Because her parents were too occupied in their own personal issues to really notice her absences, Anna began to feel more comfortable with spending more and more time with Jonathan. Ironically, as her parent's relationship deteriorated, her relationship with Jonathan flourished. However, Anna soon learned the lesson that is true for most things in life: when something seems too good to be true, it usually is. One afternoon, Jonathan left Anna alone at his house while he ran a quick errand. While he was gone, she decided to tidy up the house and found his checkbook. She became confused when she found that Jonathan was making townhouse payments to a Sapphire Taylor.

Anna, a young woman who possessed intelligence and strength, decided to not only confront Jonathan but to also do so after obtaining more evidence. When he returned, she pretended as if she knew nothing. However, she made a mental note of the dates the checks were written from the check register. They were always written on the same day of the month: the 12th. As Anna reflected back on the past several months, she realized that he never spent time with her on the 12th. She recalled that he always gave an excuse that prevented them from being together, or either one or both of their schedules caused a conflict. She decided that she wanted to witness for herself what Jonathan did on the 12th of the month. She knew that her eyes didn't lie like most men, which many of them, often are prone to do.

When Jonathan came home, Anna internalized her anguish over knowing that the love of her life was paying for another woman's housing. Exactly how long had he been cheating on her? Who was this woman? Was he protected when he had sex with her? How old was she? Did she love him? Did he really love her? Was everything between them a lie? When he touched her, was that a lie? She wanted to blow her cover and confront him, but she decided against it. It was best for her to bide her time and wait a few days to see for herself; she knew needed to exercise patience. Anna was extremely intelligent, but she was not a great actress. Because of this, Jonathan noticed a change in her demeanor. "What's wrong, Ma?"

"Nothing." Anna frowned.

"I know better than that. Talk to me; you're barely even looking at me."

"I just have a lot on my mind."

"Like what?"

She had to think quickly and play her hand with precision. "My parents; I think they are seriously headed for a divorce."

"But that's a good thing, right? They are miserable together."

"I know, but I still love them, and things will be so different not seeing them together."

"You know whatever happens between them, I'm here Ma."

"I know. Part of me is just so mad."

"Why?"

"Because my father is a cheating bastard and I still love him. I don't think men realize the affect cheating has on their families; especially on the women they cheat on."

Turning away from her, he sighed. "I think some men have an idea."

"I think men and women love differently."

"I don't."

"I know my mother could never cheat on my father. She loves him and has put up with so much for so long. My father has been so cruel, so heartless. I've seen so much growing up…I could write a book. Why are men like that? Why do men do such terrible things when they have everything they need at home?"

"I think it's because some men get weak. It has nothing to do with their love; it's a matter of the physical curiosities. Ma, some men make mistakes that they regret and will regret for a lifetime."

"If a man loves someone, then their love should stop them from doing something that could cost them that love. If anything, men shouldn't put themselves in a situation where they would be in a predicament where that problem would even arise."

"So you're saying that if a man cheats once that there is no room for forgiveness?"

"None…" Anna retorted sadly.

The two were silent. The dialogue between them told one another more than they knew. For Jonathan, it added to his anxiety. He loved her; she was his life and he needed her in his life. He wanted to see her through her college years and make a home with her. He longed for her to one day be his wife. He wanted children with her. He needed to destroy the threat to his life with the woman he loved; that threat was the one mistake he regretted in his life: Sapphire Taylor. For Anna, she spoke with growing resentment towards men. She simultaneously felt the pain of a woman who sensed the deception of a lover who has destroyed her trust. She loved him and couldn't imagine her life without him. He was indeed her prince; her exotic and erotic 'Papi'. She hoped against hope. She refused to fall victim to the common and vicious cycle of women who stayed in relationships with men who couldn't remain faithful. She needed to remain strong and resolute, and at the very least, she needed to tell herself that she could remain that way…even if it was a lie. Even with the betrayal she felt, she knew that there was something about Jonathan that was different, and that there was something she needed to wait until the 12th to see.

CHAPTER 20

Elise, being extremely determined to enact revenge on Professor Langston for the 'murder' of her mother, decided to systematically destroy him. She regarded her mother's diary as if it were her personal Bible. While sitting in her living room one morning, she read the passages, reread them, and then sat down at her computer. She typed furiously, ignoring repeated calls from her job as well as knocks at her door. She created multiple files consisting of names, dates, and the severity of laws that were broken. The last file she created was titled Joan Langston. Feeling a sense of accomplishment, she began to print all of the files she created. While the files were printing, she picked up the phone and dialed seven digits.

"Professor Langston's office. This is Shirley, how may I help you?"

"This is Elise Conroy, I was wondering if you could be so kind and do me a favor?"

"How can I help you?"

"I don't know if you are aware, but you are my mother's replacement."

"I did hear about what happened, I'm so sorry," she spoke in a whisper.

"Thanks, I really appreciate that. I was wondering if you could possibly give me Joan's number. I wanted to personally thank her for all that she's done for me to help me get through this hard time. I lost my cell phone and I really need to contact her. This would mean the world to me and my mother."

"I hope you understand, but I could get in a lot of trouble for doing that."

"How old are you, dear?"

"19."

"No one will ever know you gave it to me. You would be doing me the biggest favor in the world. I couldn't begin to thank you enough."

"Well, I guess that is true. I couldn't imagine what you must be going through; especially from what Professor Langston said, you know, how your mother became so unglued and all."

Elise bit her tongue and waited for the girl to give her the number. "Thanks for nothing, bitch!" she snapped, slamming the phone down. She thought to herself that it was bad enough that this man murdered her mother, but he now had the audacity to badmouth her to strangers. What else had he said about her? Did he take delight in her death? Did he even care? "This muthafucker has to pay," she growled as she began to dial the number.

"Hello?"

"Is this Joan Langston?"

"Yes it is. Who is this?"

"That will become clear once we meet."

"Again, I'll ask, who is this?"

"I have some information about your husband that I think you may find of interest."

"What kind of information?"

"Meet me at Rose's Gourmet Coffee on Madison Avenue. Tomorrow, at noon, don't be late."

"Who are you?"

Click...

Elise smiled with contentment knowing that her plan was underway. She would indeed have her revenge!

CHAPTER 21

Tailing her boyfriend, Anna followed Jonathan. She watched as he rang the buzzer to be let in to a luxury townhouse by a scantily dressed, strikingly beautiful woman. It was all Anna needed to see; she couldn't internalize her emotions any longer and she waited outside of the townhouse to see how long it would take for him to leave. Every minute that passed seemed to be an eternity in her mind, and this only fueled her rising anger and pain. After nearly thirty minutes, he exited the townhouse visibly angry, and this prompted her to exit her car.

"So, this is the bitch you're cheating with?"

"Anna?"

"How long have you been fucking this bitch and paying for her townhouse?"

"Mama, what are you doing here?"

"*I'm* asking the muthafucking questions! How long?"

As the two quarreled, Sapphire peered through the window. With a smirk, she thought to herself, *Damn, this payday really is officially over.* She closed her curtain and left the lovers in their quarrel.

"Ma, I'm so sorry."

"Answer me, Jon!" she screamed.

"It only happened once."

"You expect me to believe that shit? You've been paying that whore. You've paid her thousands of dollars. Why the fuck do you think I'd believe it only happened once? Am I stupid to you? Was she that good?"

"Ma, I'm not lying. It only happened once. I came here tonight to give her this one last payment and told her to leave me alone..."

"What? You sound stupid as hell."

"It's seriously not what it looks like; you have to let me explain."

"What I have to do is get the hell away from you. You never loved me."

"I do love you; I'd die for you, believe me. I'm so sorry..." he professed while they looked at each other with tears in their eyes.

"If you loved me, you wouldn't have destroyed us over a really expensive one night fuck!"

"Damn it, Anna Langston! I can't lose you; not like this." He grabbed her and sobbed, "Ma, please let me explain to you the whole truth. I'll tell you everything from the beginning."

With everything she had left within her, she pulled herself away from him and slapped him. "You've already lost me, you bastard." She turned and ran to her car, no longer holding in her feelings, crying with the full exposure of her hurt and pain revealed to him. He ran after her, but he stumbled over a rock. The stumble proved to give Anna the time she needed to get into her car and lock the doors.

Trying in vain to open the car door, he screamed, "Anna! Mama please, you're my life. Don't leave me. I'll die without you. Please let me explain. You don't know everything." She pushed the ignition button on her car and sped off. Jonathan dropped to his knees crying, "Ma, you don't know... it's your father..."

While driving home, Anna called her mother, the first person she could think of to call. "Mom?"

"Baby, what's wrong?"

"I have something to tell you."

"Where are you?"

"Mommy, he hurt me."

"Oh my God, baby, where are you?"

"I'm driving home."

"Who hurt you? What happened?"

"Jonathan."

"Who is Jonathan?"

"He's someone I've been seeing for a year and a half."

"You've been seeing someone?"

"Yes."

"What did he do to you?"

"He cheated on me."

"Baby, you get here and we'll finish this. As you know, I've been there more times than I care to remember."

For a brief moment, Anna felt comforted knowing that her mother would be able to share in her pain and would be able to aid her in seeing her through her troubles. When she got home, she was met with tenderness and understanding. Her mother didn't berate her for hiding her relationship; she told her that she understood why she hid it. Joan wanted her daughter, from that moment forward, to feel comfortable coming to her for any and everything. She also told Anna about the changes that would be taking place. She gave her daughter words of encouragement, and detailed accounts of how she got through the countless acts of betrayal she suffered at the hands of her father.

"Mommy, why? Why did you stay so long?"

"Because I loved him, and part of me felt as if I deserved it because I couldn't give him more children. I was insecure, and over time, I lost sight of what I wanted in life and began to live for him. I ignored my wants, needs, and self-worth."

"I love him so much, and I believe him when he says he loves me, but how could he do it? He kept saying there was so much that I didn't know."

"Right now things are still raw. I can't and won't tell you what to do. I trust the young woman I raised. Follow your heart, and never allow yourself to be anyone's doormat. Always go through life with your eyes open."

"He was paying for this woman's townhouse. Her name is Sapphire. Sounds like a stripper's name, doesn't it?" She tried to force a laugh through her pain.

"I'd have to say so," Joan responded with a laugh hugging her daughter. "Find out as much as you can. That's my advice. You also need to sleep on it."

Mother cradled daughter in her arms and rocked her as she once did when she was little. Joan knew that things had to be different; seeing her daughter in pain reinforced in her mind that it was imperative that she secure a comfortable life for she and her daughter when the dust settled. Anna's phone began to ring, and Joan saw that it was a call from Jonathan. Joan simply turned off the phone and continued to hold her crying baby.

CHAPTER 22

The following day, Joan called Jason and informed him of her impending meeting with the anonymous caller. He informed her that he and Chris would also meet her there because they had information for her regarding the sonogram photo. After her discussion with Jason, Joan decided to tell Anna about the envelopes and how she planned on officially ending the marriage. Anna told her mother that she supported her decision and that her father deserved to be alone based upon his behavior.

"Mommy, I'm going with you. You don't know who this woman is and you're not going alone."

"Jason and Chris are going to meet me there. I'm not going to be alone."

"Me and you against the world, right?" she questioned with a wink.

"You know I could never say no to you."

"Plus, if this woman has information that is going to help you get the answers to the questions you have regarding Daddy, then I need to be there to support you. I'll be there for you like you were for me last night."

"Well, if you're going, we have to get going now; we have to be there by noon."

"Okay, well let me just put on my sweats, you know, just in case I have to whip her ass."

"Anna!"

"I'm sorry, Mommy, but I'm serious."

"Listen, you're coming, but I'm the one doing all the talking; do you understand me?

"Yes, I understand."

The ride to meet the phantom caller was done in silence. The two women had so many thoughts floating about their heads. Joan thought about truth, liberation, the vast unknown of the future, and about her daughter. Anna, on the other hand, thought about the dissolution of her parents' marriage and her relationship with Jonathan. He called her some sixteen times and left nine messages, none of which she checked. She didn't have the heart to listen to his pleas and she didn't particularly like her mother's advice of 'listening to her heart'. She wanted to be told to never talk to him again; it would have made things easier because she really wanted to be held in his arms. She truly missed him.

Both women watched cars pass and pedestrians amble over crosswalks while feeling an increased sense of anxiety about their meeting with the mystery caller. Once they arrived at Rose's Gourmet Coffee, they noticed Jason and Chris sitting at a booth towards the front of the shop, but they didn't acknowledge their presence. They chose to sit at a booth directly across from the men, and a thin, blonde waitress walked over. "Welcome to Rose's, can I start you off with our coffee of the day?"

"We'll both have a cup of green tea with two Equals please," Joan replied.

Looking around the shop, Anna noticed when Elise walked in. "Mom, that's Saara's daughter over there."

"Are you sure?"

"Yes, that's the woman from the news."

Elise stood at the door momentarily, then looked straight at Joan and Anna and proceeded to make her way towards them. Once she reached her targets, she looked them both in the eyes. "May I have a seat?"

"Of course," Joan replied politely.

"I didn't assume you'd be bringing your daughter with you," she said, looking at Anna.

"How did you know this was my daughter?" Joan said defensively.

"Don't worry, Mrs. Langston… May I call you Joan?" she asked, not waiting for Joan's response. "I have no problem with you. My problem is with your husband. See, he killed my mother."

"Excuse me?" Joan questioned sarcastically.

"You've met my mother several times. I'm Saara Conroy's daughter, Elise."

"We know who you are!" Anna interjected.

"What did I tell you, Anna?" Joan snapped.

"How exactly did my husband kill your mother when it was clearly a suicide? I hope you didn't call me here to waste my time."

"No… By no means, Joan," she replied smugly. "Quite the contrary… What I have to tell you, and you, Anna, will prove to be life-changing."

"How so?"

"Does the name Sapphire Taylor mean anything to you, Joan?"

"Yes!" Anna blurted, unable to hide her emotion.

Puzzled that Anna knew the name, she continued with her story. "Well, Joan, your husband is in love with her. Your husband, in addition to sleeping with a number of his students, fell in love with this woman. His love for this woman consumed him so much that he began treating my mother so badly and with so much contempt that he fired her, which drove her to her death."

Anna sat, paralyzed, listening to Elise. That name kept repeating in her mind: *Sapphire Taylor, Sapphire Taylor, Sapphire Taylor.*

"How do I know you're not making this up?" Joan asked.

"As you know, my mother spent an incredible amount of time with your husband over the past eight years. She kept a detailed diary that he knew nothing about. My mother was very good about detailing things; it was a little something she learned in therapy many, many moons ago. She knew things about your husband that no one knew." She then turned to Anna, "She also knew about the relationship that you believed was a secret. I believe his name is Jonathan Torres? Yes, that's it. Daddy knew all about it and has been following you for quite some time."

Joan and Anna looked at each other with expressions of shock and fear written all over their faces. "That son of a *bitch*!" Joan hissed through her clenched teeth.

"How could he?" Anna moaned, shaking her head.

"Well, I think my job here is done. I think I gave you ladies enough to chew on for now. Joan, if you would be so kind as to give me your e-mail address; I'll forward you more specifics from my mother's diary."

"I'd appreciate that, even though I think your motive is more to hurt my husband than it is to help our family," Joan noted with a tone indicating her seriousness. She took a piece of paper and a pen from her designer purse and scribbled the information down quickly.

"Well, you ladies have a pleasant evening. Check your inbox in a few days. My work on your husband is not done." She got up and exited the same way she entered: looking like a determined woman on a mission.

As Jason and Chris saw Elise leave, they walked over to Joan and Anna's table.

"Jonathan!" Anna said, with a long pause. "Mommy, can I take the car? I need to go see Jonathan. I have to go talk to him."

"Go ahead, baby. I completely understand. Just be careful." Joan hugged and kissed her daughter. Anna then proceeded to give Jason a hug and she waved at Chris while exiting with urgency.

Joan, trying to digest the gravity of the news she just received, simply repeated, "That son of a *bitch*!"

"Girl, what happened? What did she say?" Jason questioned as he and Chris took a seat next to her.

"Joan, you're not looking so good. Let me go get you some water," Chris offered as he got up to leave the table to obtain a fresh glass of water.

"That son of a bitch… I knew he was evil… I knew he was fucking other women… But I'd *never* thought he'd fall in *love* with another woman."

"Fall in love? Does he even know the meaning of the word? Who was that woman? She looked awfully familiar."

"That was Elise Conroy, Saara Conroy's daughter. Saara was Greg's former secretary and personal assistant." Chris returned, holding a glass of ice water. "Thank you, Chris," she forced a smile, accepting the glass of water.

"She not only told me that her mother kept a detailed diary of all of Greg's infidelities, but that she also wrote about all of his dirt. He is in love with a student of his, and not to mention, he's been following Anna!"

"Your husband needs serious help; what's wrong with him?" Christopher interjected.

"Amen to that!" Jason agreed.

"You mean soon-to-be-ex-husband." Joan firmly announced.

"Did she tell you who the bitch is?" Jason questioned.

"She said the girl's name is Sapphire T-a-y-l-o-r...." Joan recalled with hesitation. "Oh Shit! Why didn't I catch that? Sapphire Taylor is the name of the woman Anna's boyfriend was seeing. Oh my God. I bet that son of bitch had something to do with this."

"Since when did Anna have a man?" Jason asked with surprise.

"It's a long story, but that bitch was seeing the both of them. I seriously don't have a good feeling about any of this."

Joan picked up her cell phone and dialed Anna's number, however, the call went straight to her voicemail. "Damn. Anna, this is Mommy. Call me as soon as you get this message. I need to talk to you. Please let me know you're okay." She pressed the button to end the call.

"Don't worry Joan; I'm sure Anna will be okay. You know the baby you raised has turned out to be one fiercely strong young woman," Jason reassured her. Turning to Christopher, he joked, "I still can't believe she got a man. I need to see this one."

"I hope you're right." Joan sighed, trying to lessen her concern.

Chris sensed Joan's worry and decided that it was a good time to share the information he found. "Joan, I was able to find out some information regarding that sonogram photo. I was able to have some of my colleagues who are OB/GYNs at several local hospitals, as well as the clinic at your husband's University, cross-reference the identification numbers found on the sonogram. The findings were quite interesting. As you know, the last two digits were missing, so that made it quite difficult to get a positive identification, but we now have a lead. The sequence of numbers found on that sonogram only comes from patients seen at the University Health Clinic. Unfortunately I don't have patient name, but we are certain of the place the sonogram photo came from," Chris's strong voice affirmed with confidence.

"This is starting to make more and more sense. Chris, I don't know how I can begin to thank you."

"You know at the end of the day, we got you," Jason avowed, grabbing Joan's hand.

"No thanks needed, Joan," Chris reassured her sympathetically.

"We need to find out more about this Sapphire Taylor. The fact that this bitch is fucking Greg and Anna's boyfriend is not sitting right with my spirit. Then I get the pregnancy test and the sonogram photo. Anna was so confident that her boyfriend was different than most of these men out here; she is a great judge of character. My Momma always told me, 'Follow your first mind' and my mind is telling me this woman is up to no good; it's more than a coincidence. As far as Greg's concerned, I'm going to take his ass down if it's the last thing I do."

Jason and Christopher looked at each other, then back at Joan. They saw before them a woman who was finally releasing the strength that laid dormant inside of her throughout all the years she spent trying to be the perfect wife. Joan no longer needed Jason to provide her with words of encouragement; she no longer needed others to have the backbone that she should have had for herself. Joan was now the woman she should have been when she would cower in her room and cry. She had nothing left to lose; but she had the world to gain. It was clear that she had now developed a thirst for life, and that thirst would prove to be insatiable.

CHAPTER 23

The quarrel between two lovers can be a fierce battle of wills, but this wasn't the case with Anna and Jonathan. Anna and Jonathan's relationship was far more than an extremely attractive man and his beautiful younger girlfriend entangled in the everyday drama that frequently ends relationships. Anna and Jonathan's battle was for the salvation of a love that transcended their age difference, and this transcendence surpassed even his monumental error in judgment. When the two met, they left their egos at the door and allowed their hearts to drive their discourse.

As Anna and Jonathan gazed at one another, tears saturated their eyes. He recounted the final encounter between him and Sapphire.

"When you sent me that text, I was with Anna. You know this has to stop!"

"I'll stop when I tell you it's time to stop, and not a moment sooner," Sapphire hissed with a sinister grin.

"You never did tell me how you knew about me, and it's clear, Ma, that your problem is not with me. You have a bigger motive in all of this - what is it? Why the fuck are you hell bent on ruining me and my Anna?"

"You honestly think I give a flying fuck about you and your little bitch? Get real. I care about the money. If you were a stronger man, you would have turned me down. Did you turn me down? No! So don't act like you're a victim. You don't have the right to play the victim; you make more than enough to keep me on the payroll, and again, my silence is priceless."

"Priceless? Aye, dios mio. Tu estas loca! You honestly think I should continue to pay you forever over one night?"

"You're damn right!"

"Hell no!"

"Then little Anna will just have to know how you used that 'magnum' on me. I'll have to detail for her how I took inch by beautiful inch of what do you call it, 'pinga'?"

"Not before I tell her myself. I love Anna and I don't know where you came from or who put you up to this, but I'd rather her hear about this mistake from me rather than from a bitch like you."

"Bitch? You better hold your tongue. You're sealing your fate, Mr. Torres."

"You know what's really sad? You're blackmailing me, and even though I did make the mistake of fucking you, you couldn't even come close to understanding what I have with Anna. You couldn't understand what I feel for her. Anna is my world and you think you can just snap your fingers and come between us? You're fucking sick!"

"I'll show you how sick I am. Get your Puerto Rican ass out my house and leave the check on the table."

"Puta sucia! I'm not going anywhere. I want to know how you know so much about me. Trust me, I'm going to tell Anna about us myself; your gravy train is over, bitch. I'm not giving you another fucking dime. If you want money, I suggest your sleezy ass go get a job. Who told you about me? Who put you up to this?"

"*I said, get the fuck out!*" Sapphire screamed, showing more anger than she intended to.

"I'm not leaving until you tell me the truth."

"You sure you want to know? You sure you can handle it?" Feeling that she had lost the security of the money she was extorting from him, she took pleasure in the satisfaction that the truth that she would reveal would deal one final blow. "If you insist, then I'll tell you. I know so much about you because I heard it from the man who you think knows nothing about you; Anna's father…"

In a state of shock, Jonathan turned from Sapphire, who was staring at him with a smile on her face indicating that she was truly satisfied with what she had done. He exited her townhouse without another word.

Holding one another, Jonathan pulled his beloved Anna closer to his heart. As he finished his story, he emphatically told her how sorry he was that he ever let her down.

"It's okay. I know we can get through this and I don't think this is entirely your fault. While my father has known about us for quite some time, there is more to the story than you know."

"Like what?" Jonathan questioned.

"Sapphire is the woman my father has been having an affair with."

"No!" Jonathan exclaimed in astonishment.

"Yes! My father has been following us the whole time. He knew everything from the beginning." As Jonathan continued to hold the woman he loved, words escaped her mouth that sent chills down his spine and frightened him, "Daddy…he brought that bitch into our lives and they both have to pay; one way or another…"

CHAPTER 24

Joan, sleeping heavily and alone in her king-sized bed, found herself awakened by screams that seemed to come from the foyer. "Mommy, come quick! Hurry up!"

Joan, startled and stumbling out of the bed, made a hasty exit out of the room and ran towards the screams of her only child. "What's wrong, baby? What is it?"

Jumping up and down, Anna screamed, "I got in! I got in! Harvard and Brown! Full academic scholarships to both; I can't believe it!"

"I thought something was wrong…you scared me to death!" Joan panted, holding her chest trying to calm her breathing.

"No, nothing is wrong Mommy, everything is right! Mommy…its Brown, its Harvard! Not bad for number two, is it?" Anna's joy radiated from her smile.

Joan knew there would be no way that she could dwell on the personal tumultuousness of her marriage; this was her daughter's moment and she needed to relish in that. "I'm so proud of you. You've worked so hard," Joan beamed while hugging her daughter. "You have such a big choice ahead of you, but between the two, it's a great choice to have."

"I know! They were my number one and number two choices. At least I don't have to worry you about tuition. Mommy, I have to call Jonathan!" Anna hugged her mother again tightly and ran upstairs to her room.

Joan stood there momentarily, taking in the bittersweet moment. She remembered, years ago, when she and Gregory discussed what it would be like to experience their only child getting her first college acceptance letter. Here, the time had come; two letters in the same day from two of the most prestigious institutions in the country. Joan's baby girl was soon to spread her wings, and she was going to be alone.

Alone is how Joan had become accustomed to sleeping for the past several weeks. Anna had found love. Her boyfriend was older than Joan would have liked; however, she knew deep within, call it her motherly instinct, that Anna had a keen sense of judgment. The numerous, candid conversations they shared since their meeting with Elise confirmed for her that what Anna and Jonathan shared was genuine. His one act of infidelity, while wrong, could be overcome and they could continue to have a happy life together.

Joan saw change all around her. Jason and Dr. Christopher Stevens were inseparable; the two were experiencing something that went far beyond the physical. Jason's face would light up with schoolboy glee at the mention of the man who touched him in ways that no man ever had before.

Joan eventually walked to her bedroom and sat down before her mirror. Looking into the glass, she saw reflections of nights where she would lay across the bed behind her and cry herself to sleep. She relived, night after night, of lying awake hoping and longing for a husband who would never show. She opened the vanity drawer and took out a pair of scissors, took her hair out of her ponytail, and let it fall beyond her shoulders. "Change, change, change..." Joan kept whispering to herself, and before she knew it, her beautiful locks began to land on the floor.

CHAPTER 25

The male ego is said to be a fragile thing. But Gregory Langston's ego, however, was as strong as steel. No matter how wrong he may be in any given situation, he will never flinch or admit fault. He is a master of manipulation, finding and exploiting weakness and using it to his advantage. One of the attributing factors to Gregory's bravado was the fact that he always maintained a sense of control, that is, until he met Sapphire. Sapphire was the kryptonite that weakened the man of steel.

"I've been calling you for the past two hours…where have you been? I was ready to come over," Gregory spoke, showing a slight amount of frustration.

"That wouldn't have been a good idea; I was too busy to be bothered with the phone."

"Busy doing what that you couldn't take my call? I'm aimlessly driving around the city. I don't feel like going back home to my bitch of a wife."

"Does it really make a difference why I didn't answer the phone?" Sapphire questioned sarcastically. "You can come over now if you want, I'm very eager to see you. I just got out of the shower and I need you to help me dry off," her words painted an image in his mind that gave his manhood an instant rise.

"I'm eager to see you too, baby."

Gregory, with no regard for the other drivers on the road, maneuvered a U-turn to head towards his impending night between the legs of Sapphire. No sooner than twenty minutes after the two ended their conversation, Gregory arrived at Sapphire's townhouse. He rapped on the door with three enthusiastic knocks, and to his welcomed surprise, she answered the door fully nude. "Come in."

Immediately, he grabbed the back of her head and pressed his lips to hers. She returned the kiss with intensity, allowing a moan to escape. He slid his hands down and groped her firm, round ass, squeezing it with vigor while lifting her into his arms and walking towards the couch. The two, so lost in the moment, never even bothered to close the door behind them. Like a wild woman, she removed the Burberry tie he wore and ripped his shirt from his body, beginning to bite and lick on his nipples. Gregory winced from both pleasure and pain. Sapphire, being the pro that she was, knew exactly what he liked and used it to her advantage. She wrapped her legs around his waist, unfastened his belt, and unbuckled his pants. "Please fuck me," she whispered while slowly pushing his pants down.

Gregory slowly entered Sapphire, feeling the warm sweetness of her orifice. She'd learned many tricks, and this night, she decided to use one in particular on the professor. She wrapped one leg around his waist and locked it. She then twirled and gyrated her pelvis, flexing her pussy up and down the length of his shaft. Gregory tried for as long as he could to resist the eruption that was inevitable, but it was to no avail. When he tried to pull himself out of her, she'd grip him even harder. "Give it to me, Daddy. Make me feel it."

"God damn you girl!" he moaned as he erupted inside her sweetness, collapsing his full weight upon her. Sapphire laid under him; her mind swirled with thoughts of what this act of sexual indiscretion would secure for her. Gregory's thoughts were, however, vastly different. They both became still and silent, lost in their thoughts for the moment. Then, the silence was broken by Gregory. "I'm ready to leave my wife."

"What?"

"I'm ready to leave my wife. You and I make much more sense. We connect in a way that I find hard to begin to articulate."

Did something happen?" she asked with frustration.

"I'd thought you'd be a bit more excited about the idea."

"It's not that I'm not excited, but this seems to be coming out of the blue."

"No, it's that when a man gets to a certain age, he doesn't need a shitload of baggage in his life and you make me feel young. You make me feel like there is nothing I can't do; it's like I know what love is again."

When he mentioned that four-letter word to her, chills raced down the length of her spine. She didn't know what else to say, but the truth escaped from her mouth: "I'm pregnant!" While the two continued to dialogue, little did they know that their act of adultery was being witnessed by an onlooker from the shadows. The onlooker had an axe to grind and wouldn't be satisfied until vengeance had been achieved.

CHAPTER 26

Many times, the simplest acts can be the most freeing. For some people, the act can be a kind gesture to a stranger. It can also be a cathartic expression through poetry or something as simple as keeping a journal. When thinking about her mother, Elise hoped that Saara found the peace in death that she didn't have in life. Saara was known for keeping detailed notes on everything that happened throughout her life. After reading through her diary, Elise strongly believed that the root cause to her mother's death fell squarely at the feet of Professor Langston. Exposing a portion of what she knew about him to his wife and daughter was only the first part of her plan of revenge. Elise was bound to ruin the Professor; she needed a plan of action to further destroy him. How was she going to do it?

Holding her mother's diary, she sat down at her computer and flipped to a page towards the end. While reading it, she thought to herself, *That's it!* She opened her e-mail, typed Joan's address in the recipient field, and feverishly composed a message that would commence the second phase of her plan. She began the message by copying the entry she read in the journal:

I found out some more juicy information about that tramp. She's been scraped more times than a Chinese woman scrapes the feet of ghetto bitches at a nail salon. I did a little digging into this Sapphire Taylor's background - well, as much as I could find. Come to find out, she has had three abortions at the University clinic. One night, Gregory told me to leave work early and wouldn't give me an explanation why. Well, on my way home I remembered I had forgotten my medication in my desk drawer, so I turned around. When I got back to the office, I heard a woman talking, so I decided to listen before I entered. I heard her saying, "What do you mean it's too late? I'm not even showing!" My cell phone rang and clearly startled her, because I could hear her hang up the phone. So then I entered the room, and who do I see? None other than Sapphire Taylor, the bitch who is trying to take the man I love. She had the nerve to ask me what the fuck I was doing there. Can you believe it? She was so incredibly rude to me. Well, I held firm to the notion that women should always have a certain level of class, so I just walked over, excused myself, got my medication, and left. Can this be Gregory's baby? It can't be. It just can't be. I have to try to do it. I have to know if I have a chance. It's do or die.

Joan, this is the second to last entry in my mother's diary. I don't know whether or not that bitch has told Gregory that she is knocked up, but my mother knew deep down inside, and she humiliated herself trying to win your husband's affections. I think you and I need to have another meeting. I have something else I'd like to discuss with you. You have my number. Use it!

Elise Conroy

CHAPTER 27

Independence. It can be a woman's best friend, especially when she's been emotionally incarcerated and the warden is a Langston. Now there was no way that Joan could go back to living the life she once knew. She now breathed life; she drank it in and now had acquired a taste for it. She arrived at the Langston estate with several bags in hand while sporting a new asymmetrical haircut: hair tapered in the back and chin-length in the front. Joan loved the way her new cut sculpted her face. She began to look at herself in the mirror and truly appreciate how much beauty she possessed for a woman her age. *Damn Joan, you do still have it,* she thought to herself.

New clothes, check; new cut, check; and tomorrow I reclaim the world! Joan laughed to herself. She turned from the mirror and sat down at her computer to begin constructing a 'want ad'. While beginning to detail the specifics of the advertisement, she heard the front door open. Assuming it was Anna, she yelled, "Baby, come here! I want to show you something…I have a surprise for you!" Joan kept typing away as she heard steps ascend the stairs and draw closer to her room.

"What the hell did you do to your hair?"

Startled, but not showing it, she ignored his question and greeted him. "Hello to you too, Greg."

"Answer me. Why did you cut your hair? It's not very becoming."

Without even turning around, she asked, "Is there a reason why you are here? You haven't been here in weeks, and then you come here to offer an opinion about my hair that I didn't ask for."

"You know I know what's best and you need to always separate yourself from being compared to the typical Black woman. Short hair is too Black."

Turning around, showing her frustration without care of hiding it anymore, she responded, "I honestly didn't ask you what your opinion is, nor do I care. You have the audacity to walk in here and critique my looks? I'll ask you again, why the fuck are you here?"

"I'm leaving you, that's why I'm here. You haven't been the wife that I've wanted for years and I'm done with you. You're a disappointment. I've wanted more children, couldn't get 'em from you, and now I'm with someone who can give me everything I need and more."

"Is that what you want?"

"Yes."

Standing up and walking over to him, she found the strength to say the words she hadn't ever had the courage to utter to her husband: "Well, this is something I will not fight you on. But before you leave, we need to get some things straight first. You can continually throw in my face the fact that I can't have any more children - but you know what, Greg? I thank God for the one child we do have together who, for your information, has just gotten a free ride to both Brown and Harvard, Mr.-Father-of-the-Year! I'm glad I don't have any other children by you because you are the worst kind of man; you actually disgust me. You think because you work doing what you do and that because *WE* have money in the bank that it makes you God. Greg, you're not God nor are you better than anyone else. What the fuck is wrong with you? You've been fucking other women and I've turned a blind eye because I loved you…because I believed that I needed you. Truth of the matter is: you ain't shit and I don't want you. As far as I see it, we haven't had a marriage for years and it's time I moved on."

With a condescending chuckle, Greg replied, "Brown and Harvard, huh…and she didn't even bother to call me? That damn ingrate. She owes her success to me and not even a damn phone call. You two could never give me the appreciation that's due - you two are cut from the same cloth. I suggest you get a lawyer; I'll be contacting one in the morning."

"Anna doesn't owe you shit! The only thing she owes you is a kick in the ass for being so overbearing and controlling, but you'd never see that. You're stuck in your ways." She paused momentarily. "Be prepared to keep me in the lifestyle to which I've grown accustomed because you seem to be forgetting something. Even though I took a backseat to you in this marriage, I came into it with just as much as you did. I helped build this showpiece of a home; I'm not one of your students, Professor Langston. You don't have rank over me and you don't give me grades. I'm no little girl that salivates over you like a bitch in heat. The last time I checked, there are several degrees that I possess but don't utilize, one of which says Ph.D."

"If you think you're so tough, then a battle we can have. Just be prepared; I don't think you're going to like the outcome, Joan."

"I think you've underestimated me for far too long."

Gregory turned and marched to his walk-in closet in silence. He packed a suitcase full of clothes, just enough to indicate that his departure wasn't permanent. Joan returned to her computer, minimized several windows, and maximized the tab that was on the lower right hand side of the monitor. After reading the screen for a second time, she closed out the window and saved her documents. Grabbing her keys and cellular phone, she headed out to her car, leaving Gregory there alone.

CHAPTER 28

Most people fundamentally believe that truth and honesty are paramount to obtaining happiness. But if one was to consider Gregory Langston, for example, these paramounts would not apply. Being an extremely attractive, highly educated, well-paid, established middle aged gentleman, he is willing to forsake his marriage for a woman that, he believes, loves him. In his mind, what she tells him is the truth. When he is with the striking Sapphire Taylor, nothing matters. Would the truth, the real truth, bring him happiness? Would he regret allowing love to blind him? Will the truth be too much for him to bear?

"I did it; I told her that I was leaving her and that she should look for a lawyer."

"What did she say when you told her I was pregnant?" Sapphire quizzed.

"I didn't tell her that."

"What do you mean you didn't tell her?" Sapphire, again, was growing visibly irritated.

"It's not going to be that easy."

"Why the fuck not, Gregory?"

"Because we've been married for over twenty years. For God's sake, use your brain! I can't very well go into court with a pregnant girlfriend. Do you want her to take me for everything I have? I have to play this the right way. You have to trust me, baby."

Pretending to submit to his act of being assertive, she apologized. "I'm sorry Daddy, I wasn't thinking. I just want to make sure that our child has the best. The best would be for us to all be together, and my townhouse is not the place for us to do that. Your estate is where we should be, so your wife has to go. Promise me you'll make that happen," she whined in a syrupy sweet voice while walking towards him. Sitting next to him on her couch, she rests her head on his shoulder and then begins to kiss him while massaging his crotch. "I'm sorry, Daddy. Please forgive me."

"You don't have to ask for forgiveness."

"Yes I do. Let me show you how sorry I am." As she felt a bulge stiffen in his pants, she freed his manhood and then took his offering into her mouth slowly while gazing into his eyes. Sapphire was quite skilled; she allowed his flesh to reach the back of her throat without ever having to worry about a gag-reflex. She stretched and slid her tongue around the circumference of his dick, making him moan aloud. His expressions of ecstasy only made her more active in her pursuit to achieve an ending to his oral pleasure. She began to stroke his shaft while concentrating on stimulating the mushroom-shaped head; moments later, he no longer held his orgasm. "I told you I was sorry," she repeated, wiping her mouth."

"I believe you," he replied, panting.

"Daddy, now that I know you forgive me, can I tell you something?"

"Anything in the world."

"Well, if you are going to be going through this divorce with your wife, I think it would be best that you present yourself as single. You and I need to slow things down; you know I love you. We should separate - it's only temporary."

"What?" he cried visibly confused.

"Think about it. We stand a better chance of getting more if she can't play the victim. Let's not give her that chance. We can still see each other, but it has to be in secret. I'm registered for your class for the summer session. You have to admit that it has been nice having me as a 'student' for this semester." Sapphire spoke with a smile.

"Yes it has, and I do see your point. I'll secure a condo and move there. We'll see each other in class and I'll 'tutor' you after class during my office hours, or at least until we finalize this divorce."

"Exactly! Let's work this out. Daddy, remember, you own this," Sapphire purred while grabbing his hand and placing it on the warm, wet spot between her legs. She began slowly moving her hips in a circular motion. "It will always be yours…"

Joan, just now leaving a very informative meeting, was running late for Anna's celebratory dinner. This would be the first time she was to meet the infamous Jonathan Torres; additionally, Jason and Dr. Stevens were scheduled to drop by to also give their congratulatory wishes for her acceptance into Brown and Harvard. Joan's meeting ran much longer than she had anticipated, and she felt the pressure of her tardiness while making her way across town to Azul Allure.

As life would have it, three miles from the restaurant, Joan hit a traffic jam. She reached for her phone, but the battery was dead; it died earlier that evening while she was driving to her meeting. Joan hated to be late for anything - she always valued promptness. While looking at the sea of red lights before her, she sat thinking about the meeting she just left. What would be her next move? Could she go through with it? What would all of it mean for her and her daughter in the end? Joan needed to not only focus her attention on making it to Anna's dinner, but she also needed to focus on clearing her mind of anything regarding that meeting. "Get it together Joan," she repeated to herself as she slowly pressed the accelerator, then the brakes in repeated motions; stop and go, stop and go. Joan turned up the radio to hear Monica's 'Still Standing" resonating from the speakers. *Fitting song*, Joan thought. *"After all this shit, I'm still standing, but I know who won't be.* She cast her gaze down to look at a folder she took from her meeting. Its contents contained a picture of a woman whose name is that of a gem; she had eyes that were extraordinarily blue.

"I'm so sorry I'm late; my cell phone died and I couldn't call," Joan admitted, hugging Anna.

"It's okay. Mommy, let me introduce you to Jonathan. He's been a bit nervous to meet you, but I'm sure you will make him feel comfortable," Anna retorted with a wink.

A very regal Hispanic male stood up and extended his hand to shake Joan's. "Mrs. Langston, it's a privilege to finally meet you. I see you're more beautiful in person than in the photos Anna has shown me."

Good Lord, this man is fine! Good job, baby! Joan thought to herself. "No need to try and flatter me. I already approve of you," Joan said with a laugh."

"Now that the introductions are out of the way; Jason wanted to let you know that he and his partner stopped by. He tried to call you, but your phone went straight to voicemail. They dropped off this card, and said they couldn't stay because an emergency came up. I guess they were short tonight at the hospital and Dr. Stevens was on call; there was some sort of accident. Jason said he is going to try to come back."

"Well, that would be nice, but if not, he and I will talk later. Tonight is your night and we need to celebrate. I say the three of us eat something extremely fattening."

"Mommy, you know you're the first one to watch your caloric intake."

"Yeah, I know. How about strawberry cheesecake for dessert with whipped cream on top?"

"Sounds good to me!" Jonathan laughed.

CHAPTER 29

The Lord works in ways that are mysterious to man; we need to know to never question His will, but rather, to trust in it. Our actions generally find a way to catch up with us, and we must understand that one day we will be held accountable for them. Karma is indeed a bitch.

"Miss Taylor? I'm Dr. Stevens. I'm glad to see that you are awake. I need to explain to you why you are here. You were in a pretty bad accident, and as a result, you were drifting in and out of consciousness and exhibited heavy vaginal bleeding. You were able to tell the EMS worker that you were 16 weeks pregnant before you lost consciousness completely. I'm sorry to have to tell you this, but we did everything we could. The baby didn't make it."

Sapphire sat in the hospital bed, not saying a word. She just gazed into the air. "When can I leave?"

"I'd like to keep you here at least until tomorrow for observation. Would you like for us to contact someone for you? Perhaps a family member?"

"No, I just want to get the fuck out of here. That's not so hard to understand, is it?"

"Miss Taylor, I'm sorry for your loss. However, I can't, in good conscience, agree to sign you out right now. I'm going to send in our bereavement counselor so you can talk to someone. Should you need me, just contact the nurse and I'll be here."

"Whatever."

As Dr. Stevens exited the room, he quickly stepped into the lounge, picked up his phone, and dialed Jason's number.

"One minute, ya'll, this is my future husband," Jason informed everyone, excusing himself from the table. He made his way over to the bar and answered his phone. "What's going on? How is work?"

"I don't have long to talk, but you wouldn't believe who my patient is."

"Who?"

"Sapphire Taylor."

"Get the fuck out of here!"

"You know I'm keeping it very professional right now…but I'm sad to say she just lost a child tonight."

"Well, we gotta tell Joan. I just don't know if tonight is the right night. She is so happy, and I don't want to ruin her happiness. Side-note, she is working the hell out of this fierce new cut."

"Then we'll tell her tomorrow; we'll invite her over for an afternoon cocktail. I'm being paged right now, I gotta run. Keep it warm for me until I get home."

"I love you."

"I love you more."

"Bye."

"Until later."

Shaking his head, Jason headed back to enjoy the festivities with the Langston women and Mr. Torres; in the back of his mind he knew the next day would come with particular troubles. The smile Joan was wearing today would fade tomorrow and her troubles would surface yet again.

CHAPTER 30

Self-reflection is powerful. When we afford ourselves the time to reflect on the good, bad, and ugly of this life, we can see things with a crystal clarity. That clarity could lead us to move our lives in one of two directions: towards a path of self-betterment or towards a path of self-destruction. Sapphire was no exception. While looking in the mirror at the staples used to close the wound on her forehead, she thought to herself, *Damn, I hope this doesn't scar too badly.* Sapphire's self-examination was interrupted by thunderous knocks at her townhouse door.

"Are you okay? Why didn't you call me? Is the baby okay?" a concerned Gregory questioned.

"Yes, I'm okay. The baby is fine," Sapphire lied while trying to rake her hair over the staples on her forehead.

"Thank God. I was so worried when you called me. Why didn't you call me from the hospital? You know I would have come the second you called."

"Think about it...do you think we really need it documented that you were my emergency contact? I'm sure your wife will have you followed soon, that is, if she isn't doing that already."

"I love you and I love our baby. I have to make sure that you both are okay."

"You shouldn't even be here right now. I told you I was fine...I mean...we're fine," she said with hesitation.

"I can't stay away from you. Do you know how hard it is for me to stay away from you? This is torture - all I think about is holding you. Miss Taylor, you're my drug," Gregory expressed fervently, grabbing a very sore Sapphire and holding her gently in his arms.

Sapphire was a woman accustomed to internalizing her pain, and this was a time when she drew on one of those strengths: becoming numb. She allowed Gregory to hold her and profess his love to her. Emotionally, she felt nothing. When she did allow herself to feel, the emotion she exhibited was one that was usually unexpected: rage. Sapphire, while being rocked back and forth, thought back to when she was young. While there was no scent of smoke that lingered on his clothing, her mind was brought to a place where all she could do was smell the fragrance of marijuana. In reality, he was professing his love for her, but all she could hear were grunts of the two men who robbed her of her virginity. For the first time in a long time, Sapphire noticed that her eyes, which usually remained dry, began to saturate. "You need to go now."

"Let me stay, baby."

"No. You need to leave. I'll see you tomorrow - I promise," she answered coldly.

Taken aback, he conceded, "Okay…you know I'm only a phone call away." He tried to kiss her, but she turned her head away from him.

"Tomorrow... I need to go to bed."

"Okay," Gregory sighed. He exited the townhouse feeling rejected. An overwhelming sense of concern consumed him, and now his cause for concern was for a totally different reason than when he first arrived.

"I hope this will go no further than you and I. I hate to waste my hard-earned money. Do not make me regret this, because you will rue the day you ever opened your mouth and told anyone you ever crossed paths with me."

"I won't tell anyone; you can trust me. I need this money. My son's father hasn't paid me child support in over two years, and I'm behind on my rent."

"Save your sob story - I don't give a shit. Just keep your mouth shut or your son will not have a mother at all; you got it?"

"Yes, I…I do," the young intern responded nervously.

Elise Conroy was a woman who was never the same after the 'murdering' of her mother. She took a leave of absence from her job when she received the news and fell into a deep depression. Upon finding her mother's diary, she found that she no longer had to wallow in misery, aimlessly wandering around and crying in her apartment; her discovery had given her a new-found reason to wake up in the morning. Elise was now driven by her sole focus to destroy the man who took her mother from her: Gregory Langston. He had to be stopped. To Elise, Gregory was a blight on the face of this earth and she was going to purge him from it - even if it cost her everything - no price would be too high...even her own life.

Although her back was still stiff from the car accident she initiated two days prior, she knew that her own pain was inconsequential to meeting her larger objective. Elise decided to make several photocopies of the documents that she secured from the intern at the hospital. With copies in hand, Elise was ready to enact the next phase of her plan.

"How long will it take for this to arrive?" Elise questioned.

"Because it's local, it should be there no later than Friday," The clerk at the post office replied.

"Thank you so much."

"No return address?"

"No, none necessary, but you have a great day."

Exiting the post office, Elise rummaged through her oversized pocketbook in search of her cell phone. When she arrived at her car, she found her phone and placed a call. "Hello?"

"Hello?"

"It's done," Elise said in a firm, clear tone. She promptly ended the call. Moments later, she pulled into a fast food eatery to order her lunch. After finishing her meal, she placed the phone in the bag with the trash, opened the car window, and tossed the bag into the garbage pail leaving the prepaid phone behind.

CHAPTER 31

"We didn't want to say anything to you the other night because of Anna's dinner; you were so happy. But girl, this was too important for us to keep to ourselves," Jason admitted, holding Joan's hand.

"I just don't know what to say. He actually got her pregnant?" Joan quizzed, looking at Dr. Stevens. Her facial expression showed that she was now a different woman. She was no longer a woman who needed to be cradled and shielded; Joan was now a woman who needed the hard truth. Not only was she ready for it, but she could also take it.

"I can say for a fact that she was, and *'was'* being the operative word...pregnant. Seeing her in person, and given her circumstance, her behavior was so strange. I mean, she didn't even acknowledge the loss of the baby; it's like she was either in a state of denial like I've never seen before, or she truly didn't care. She didn't want to call anyone; that fact alone also struck me. If it was his child, shouldn't she have wanted him to know?"

"Well, it's a possibility in the very least. That bastard!" Joan retorted. "Was she in a lot of pain?"

"There was a moderate level of discomfort on her end, but we kept it at bay with medications."

"It's terrible that she lost her child, but is it terrible that I can't find myself feeling any sympathy for her?"

"Hell no! My Momma always said, 'You do dirt, you get dirt.' There are some dirty bitches out there," Jason said with a note of protectiveness.

"I wonder how Greg is going to take it. I know he's been wanting a child. I wonder if she even bothered to tell him...Well, I might as well tell you both: Greg came home the other day and didn't mince words. He told me I needed to find a lawyer."

"Let me beat his ass. I swear to God, Joan, let me just beat his ass just one good time," Jason begged, standing up.

"No, he'll get what's coming to him," Joan retorted.

"What did you say?" Dr. Stevens asked Joan.

"I told him basically it's a battle I'm more than prepared to fight. He just better prepare himself to keep me in my current lifestyle. I just want you two to know I have dealt with so much. Most of which, Jason, you already know...but there's a lot you don't. I loved that man for as long as I can remember and a part of me will always love him, but I do love myself more. I love my baby girl more. I had to do things over the years I'm not very proud of. I have my secrets too, but they pale in comparison to his."

"Girl, you know we have your back no matter what!" Jason announced.

"Yes, we do. You know that I told you I can't testify in court, but whatever I can do to help, you know I will," reinforced Dr. Stevens.

"Trust me, when I need you two, I will call. You two are God-sent." Joan hugged both of them.

CHAPTER 32

The tie that binds family together is the strongest of ties. The mother-daughter bond can either be a volatile or inseparable one. Joan and Anna's relationship proved to be the latter. They forged a bond through years created by laughing, reciprocal support, tears, and the commonality of being at the receiving end of abuse from Gregory Langston.

"Family is so important, Anna. I searched my soul last night and I couldn't think of any other way."

"Mom, you know what people are going to say."

"Yes, I know. We can't be so bothered with what people think."

"You say that like it's so easy. We've been through so much - I just don't know if I want to do it at this point."

"We have to reach out and try to make it work. He's your father and he's still my husband; I have to try. He loved me once and he can love me again."

"Mom, do you know how crazy this is?"

"I know, baby, but I can't just leave it alone. I'm sure he has already contacted a lawyer - I met with one yesterday. We talked for hours and I explained to him, that in my heart, this marriage is not over .I'd rather we try to go to counseling."

"This should prove to be interesting. I just don't want to see you hurt anymore, Mom. When will we be free to just live our lives; when will we be free from all of this?

"If this works out, we will all get what we deserve."

"Why the fuck didn't you tell me?"

"I'm sorry. I just didn't know how to tell you. I didn't want to hurt you."

"Our child dies, and you couldn't bring yourself to fucking tell me. You not only denied me the opportunity to mourn, but you also denied me the opportunity to be there for you. You knew very well how much I wanted another child - how could you?"

"I'm sorry. I just didn't know how to tell you. I never lost a child before. Think about how I feel. Think about how I felt. You yelling at me is making it even worse." Sapphire had a particular way of turning on her acting skills and using them flawlessly. "What I would like to know is how you found out!"

"Not that it matters; I had to find out through the mail. Someone sent me your medical documents in the mail. I don't give a damn about how I found out, the point is, I found out and it wasn't from you. You betrayed me. What do we have without trust?"

"We can work through this. I can't get through this without you. We can still have the life we planned together. I know I was wrong for not telling you - I've never loved anyone like I love you. I never lost a child before so I've never feared disappointing someone like I did you."

"I don't like being disappointed, and it will take time for me to get over this."

"What can I do?"

"Give me time," Gregory replied coldly. He walked out of the townhouse, leaving the door open.

Closing the door, Sapphire began to calculate her next move. She knew Gregory was the key to getting everything she sought; he was her final payday. She also wondered who could have sent her medical documents to Gregory and what their motive could have been. Sapphire knew that she needed to act fast. To her, this was a game of chess, and she was not going to lose

CHAPTER 33

The sting of betrayal can be lasting, especially when the heart is crushed. Gregory, for the first time, felt a glimpse of the pain he had inflicted upon those who loved him for so many years. He wanted to be angry at Sapphire so very badly, but he couldn't. The pain that he felt crept from deep within his stomach and found its way traveling to his chest every time he thought of her. He'd try to think of other things: work, correcting last minute papers, the approaching final exams, or even the summer sessions that would soon come. There was no escape from Sapphire; her absence in his class only served to make his mind focus on his feelings for her even more. What was he going to do? He'd never been in a situation like this before; a situation where he lost control of his sense of self. He could no longer endure the mounting pressure he was experiencing.

"Class, I'm going to dismiss early today. But I want you to look over the outline for review detailed on the syllabus. I'll see you all next week," Gregory professed in his most solemn tone, He made his way to his office to place a call to Sapphire, and upon his arrival, he was informed by his secretary that a gift had arrived for him. His stoic expression began to form into a smile; he believed Sapphire was sending a token to express her love for him. Once in the privacy of his office suite, he was welcomed by a bouquet of fresh fruit: strawberries, melons, pineapple, and grapes carved and made to look like flowers. Attached to the arrangement was a card:

I know I'm the last person you would expect this from. Gregory, I did as you instructed and consulted a lawyer. I've done some soul searching and I can't allow you to walk out on us. We've built something over the past twenty-five-plus years and we can't see it die now. We were there for each other when we had nothing but a dream and twenty dollars between us. I know I could have been a better wife - I know I could have done a lot of things differently. You are a good man and I didn't value that. I can say the one thing I have never done is lie to you. Greg, you can trust this when I say it. I love you. You are the only one for me and the only man I ever want to be with. I don't want to be without you. Our house is not a home without you. I tried to be strong without you - but I know without you, I'm nothing. Anna misses her father too. She's ready to apologize. She needs you, your wisdom, and your guidance.

Come home,

Joan

Placing the letter down on his desk, Gregory sat awestruck. He had grown to love Sapphire - yet he was reminded in Joan's letter that there was a history between them that, no matter how hard he tried, he couldn't deny. There was also Anna. While his ego was strong and made him into a man who was quite stubborn, he was internally mourning the loss of a child he longed for. This made him appreciate the fact that he had someone who truly wanted to be with him. Reclining in his chair, Gregory read the words from Joan over and over again; then he thought of Sapphire and her betrayal. Was the grass necessarily greener on her side of the fence?

CHAPTER 34

"I'd like to close my account," Sapphire informed the bank teller at her local branch. She knew that sometimes, even when playing chess, the game ends in a stalemate. This semester would be her last. Once it ended, she would move to another town, transfer to another school, and amass yet another fortune from men who set themselves apart from the average street hustler. Sapphire didn't desire to research who was bound to ruin her, nor was she interested in knowing who sent Gregory the damning information. She wanted out now that her quest to obtain his estate and his fortune was crumbing before her eyes. Frankly, he wasn't worth the effort.

"This is a sizable account; may I ask why you are closing the account with us?" the teller questioned.

"It's none of your god-dammed business," Sapphire snapped. "I'll take a cashier's check, and if there is a problem, you can call the bank manager over. Now do your fucking job - I don't have time to go back and forth!"

Leaving the bank fully satisfied, with check in hand, Sapphire decided to call one of her most generous donors. "Hey baby, I was wondering, do you have a little free time for us to catch a movie or whatever?"

"For you, I'll make the time," the voice on the other line responded eagerly.

"Cheryl, I hate to be a bother. You know I love you to death, but I need you to do me a serious favor. You know I'd never call in a favor unless it was an absolute emergency. I need for you to run a check on a person's cellular activity. You know this is clearly on the DL, and it will never get back to you that you gave me the information."

"Girl, you know I don't have a problem helpin' a sista out. *Shiiit*, you helped a bitch out more times than I can count. You were the one who helped me prove my sister's husband cheated on her. The phone records that mysteriously found their way to her lawyer really helped her win against that asshole. I owe you, and whatever you need, I got you."

"I'm glad you feel that way."

"No doubt!"

"Run a check on the name Sapphire Taylor, social security number 482-47-8874. If you can't find it in our system, utilize your resources with our friends at other companies. Cross-reference her most frequent calls and compile all her biographical data."

"Damn girl! That's a lot of work, but I'm sure I can get it done. When do you think you need all of this done?"

"I need this information today. I know I can trust you to get it done."

"I'll get on it right now - you know I don't do shit on this job. Hey, when the hell you coming back to work?

"No time soon. I have to take care of some things first; but listen, I have to run. Call me when you have the info. Remember, this information is of the highest priority. I can't be connected to any of this in any way."

"Okay, I'll get back to you as soon as I get what you need."

"Thanks, Cheryl."

"No problem."

Elise hung up the phone hoping that Cheryl would confirm what her mother detailed in her diary. She needed confirmation of what she read on one of the pages in her mother's diary. Should she be able to confirm what she read, she would then be able to weave additions into the tapestry of pain that she intended to inflict upon Gregory. An excerpt on page 235 read:

Poor Gregory! He's oblivious about the murmurs of the things being said about that evil bitch. She walks around here as if she's God's gift. Damn her! Why do I have to compete with two women? His wife doesn't deserve him, and surely this slut doesn't. To be such an intelligent man, he's so damn stupid when it comes to this piece of trash. What is it about her? I hear she's been fucking or has been fucked by several of the staff here. No one has the balls to mention it around him. I wish I had the heart to tell him or warn him...spare him from being hurt by this whore. Unfortunately, he'd probably never believe me. Damn! Damn! Damn!

Elise began to smile and thought to herself, *Vengeance is mine.*

CHAPTER 35

Patience is a virtue. Those who have it find that life changes with a sense of ease, however, those who don't exercise it find that life can be a challenge. Elise, looking at her watch, found that the patience she once was able to exercise was no longer there. *Where is this bitch?* she thought to herself. Her mission needed to come to fruition, and she needed to obtain the information necessary to bring down the mighty Gregory Langston. Just as she thought she couldn't wait any longer, her contact returned her call.

"What took you so long?" Elise asked angrily.

"I was just about to call you. What you asked me to do was not necessarily an easy job to accomplish. A bitch had to put in overtime today to get it done."

"What did you find out?"

"I ran the social security number you gave me in our database, and unfortunately, she wasn't in our system. Then I called one of my girlfriends at Central Telecom and as luck would have it, that's who carries her phone service. She could only view her past three statements because in their database, if an associate needs to look for anything further back than that, they need a password from management. She discovered that there was a number Sapphire dialed once a week, every week, on the same day, around the same time."

"Were you able to find out to whom that number belonged to?"

"I'm getting to it. The number didn't match anything in her system, so I referenced it in our system, and luck would have it, I found a match. I printed out the bio info we have on the match - are you near a fax machine?"

"Fax it over to the Kinkos in Beaver Haven to the attention of 'Stella'. What's the name of the person she was calling?"

"His name is Zachary McFadden; he works for the university your mother worked for. Does that help you?"

"Immensely!"

"Do you need me to do anything else for you?"

"Yes, forget you did any of this."

"Girl, you know my lips are sealed. You know how we get down. When you get done handling your business, we need to meet up and have coffee or something; a girl's night out or some shit like that."

"That would be nice…Cheryl, let me go. Thanks again!"

"Never a problem. I'm glad I was able to help."

Hanging up the phone, Elise grabbed her keys and headed to her car to drive to Kinkos. She knew that she needed to place another important phone call, but this time, the recipient of the call would find this information to be beneficial to them. When the destruction of Gregory Langston took place, Elise intended to be front and center to witness his demise and to savor his pain like a chilled glass of Moscato.

CHAPTER 36

"Daddy, I'm so glad to see you!" Anna exclaimed while sitting up in her bed.

"I'm glad to see you too, Anna. Is there something you'd like to say to me?" Gregory asked while hugging his daughter. Internally, he relished the feeling of holding his daughter, but his pride didn't allow him to show how good it felt to hold her.

"Yes. I'm so sorry for everything I said to you. I'm sorry for disrespecting you - I owe you so much. I just don't know where to begin. There are so many things that I feel so ashamed of."

"Well, let's start from the beginning."

"I felt like I could step out of my place as a child, and I was wrong. I neglected to show you the respect that was due to you and I disregarded all that you've done for me. Without you, I wouldn't be who I am. I can't deny that. I wouldn't be fortunate enough to have the choice of selecting two of the best schools in the country right now. I interfered between you and mommy, and I shouldn't have."

"Yes, that is true. I'm glad you've recognized the error of your ways."

"Yes I have; Daddy, please forgive me!" Anna cried, tears running down her face.

"Don't cry, Anna. I do forgive you. You're the only child I have left." Catching himself, he added, "I mean, you're my only child."

"I don't want our family to be torn apart. I've been having nightmares about this. Daddy, Mommy has been trying to put on this brave face, but I know it's all an act. She misses you so much. Daddy, please don't leave. I'll do anything!" Her tears now turned into a river of sobs.

"Anna, it's not that simple."

"Why isn't it? You always said that family is the most important thing in the world. Our family can't turn out like everyone else's. We can't end up like Angela's."

"What do you mean?"

"Her parents are getting a divorce."

"Where did you hear that?"

"At first I thought it was a rumor, but then she began to come to school looking depressed…students began to talk."

"What did they say?" Gregory questioned with a vested interest.

"Basically, they said that Mrs. McFadden found out that her husband was sleeping with one of his students and she put him out. She no longer wants to be married to him. Now they are going to end up going through an ugly divorce."

"I work with him every day," he said with a note of surprise.

"That's not it - there's more. It's said that he goes to work like his home life is still intact, as if nothing is wrong. From what I hear, because Mrs. McFadden is choosing to go through with a divorce, he refuses to help pay for Angela's tuition to Yale. Yeah, Daddy, she got in to Yale. She only applied to one school, got in, and didn't get a full scholarship like I did. So now she is in a situation where she is worried about how to finance school in addition to her parents' divorce."

"I had no idea," Gregory sighed, shaking his head.

"Please, Daddy. Promise me we can work this out. I don't want to lose my family. Let's not end up like the McFaddens."

"It's not that simple; but I do promise all things will be considered."

"Thank you Daddy. Will you stay with me and keep me company like you used to when I was little?"

"Of course I will."

As Gregory held his daughter, he pondered about his life and questioned again whether or not the grass was greener with Sapphire. His conversation with his daughter truly did resonate with him. He thought about his colleague and how a marriage that seemed to be built on a solid foundation could be rocked by scandal. He was a man that placed such importance on image - yet he was becoming so reckless when it came down to Sapphire. Caution was being thrown to the wind; the guard he once had was being let down. What was happening to him? Sapphire had become more than the other occasional flings he'd entertained from students he'd slept with over the years. Could he truly build a life with her? What would happen to Joan? What would happen to Anna? If Sapphire could lie to him about something as important as the death of a child, what else was she capable of? Was having so many questions worth the gamble at this point in his life? They leaped around his mind endlessly until he noticed the subtleness of Anna's snores.

Walking into his bedroom, he noticed Joan sitting upright on the bed with her legs crossed reading a book. She wore a short red nightgown that accented the curves of her body perfectly. The front of the gown was sheer enough for him to gaze at the contour of her breasts and the outline of her nipples. He found himself breath-taken by her sheer beauty. Her beauty wasn't that of a young vixen, but it was of a woman who was simply exquisite. She was a vision. She didn't need makeup; her beauty shone without her even trying to make an effort. Why hadn't he noticed or appreciated this before? Looking up from her book, she tilted her head and asked, "Greg, how long have you been standing there?"

"I just got here."

"Did you get a chance to see Anna before she went to bed?"

"Yeah, she and I were able to bury the hatchet."

"So then that only leaves us to do the same," she smiled, walking over to him and giving him a hug.

"Look Joan…"

"Greg, I'm not prepared to let us go. Call this off. You can't tell me you don't love me."

"You know I…"

"I know you do. I can tell by the way you just looked at me. Just tell me you're not leaving and we'll work the rest out. I don't care how much time it'll take."

"Joan, I'll stay, just don't make me regret this."

"Trust me, you deserve this more than you know… Did you enjoy your fruit?"

"It was sweet."

"I'm serious about showing you how much I've changed."

"Well, there needs to be some changes," Greg said firmly.

"I agree and I will show you. I promise," Joan said pulling her husband in for a long, slow, sensual kiss.

CHAPTER 37

Two classes left, then the final exam. All he had to do was get through the week and then he'd have some time to relax his mind a little. While preparing for class to begin, his mind could only focus on what happened between he and Joan. They shared a level of intimacy that touched him in a way that actually frightened him. He told Joan that he would stay. What would the ramifications be for his relationship with Sapphire? How could he end it with her? Did he really reach the right decision? Gregory Langston knew that he needed to meet with her and today had to be the day. He couldn't put it off; the longer he waited the more the situation would worsen.

The students entered class, all but Sapphire. Gregory appeared heavily distracted, which didn't go unnoticed by his students. "Are you okay sir?" questioned an inquisitive student.

"I'm fine. It's been a long night."

The class erupted with a chorus of hoots and howls which both embarrassed the Professor and made him smile. After the outbursts died down, he regained his composure. "Settle down everybody...let's focus." The brief distraction was what Gregory needed to redirect his attention on teaching his students the content-specific material for their final exam. Midway through the class, while the students were working on their independent assignments, Sapphire entered the lecture hall. In an authoritative voice, Gregory announced, "Miss Taylor, you're extremely late. I'm going to need to see you after class. You need to get caught up on the notes that you missed when you decided not to make coming to class on time a priority."

With nothing more than a roll of the eyes, "Okay" was all that escaped from her mouth.

In the privacy and solitude of his office, Gregory began the hard work of broaching the subject of breaking off his affair with Sapphire.

"I wanted to see you...obviously not because you were late, but I think you know that.

"Yes, I know."

"I've been doing a lot of thinking."

"So have I."

"What do you mean?"

"Look Gregory, I know where this is going."

"I'm sorry, but you not telling me about our child's death called a lot into question about honesty. I need the security of knowing that, no matter what, we build this on honesty."

"Honesty? Did we start this on honesty when, from day one, you were sneaking behind your wife's back? Don't begin lecturing me about honesty, because you are not a pillar of honesty yourself!" she hissed with her voice rising.

"Let's not argue. I'm going to call off my divorce and work things out with Joan. We have too much history for us to let it go so easily. I think we got too caught up in our relationship. But, Miss Taylor, you know I'm going to miss you."

"Fuck you!"

"That's not necessary."

"You two can both go to hell."

"I have to think about my daughter. She needs me too. I have to do the right thing. Please try to understand…I'm sorry."

"Understand? You end things with me to go back to the bitch you've complained about over and over again and you expect me to simply understand? Okay…" she raked through her hair, shaking her head to indicate an affirmative answer. "Have it your way and good luck with everything."

"Will you be okay?"

"That's not your concern any longer," she responded coldly while turning from him and walking to the door. Before making her final exit, she smiled wickedly. "See you soon, Professor Langston." Even though something in her tone startled him, he breathed a sigh of relief when she exited his office.

CHAPTER 38

Satisfaction is always relative. Some find satisfaction from turning over at night and eating a morsel of chocolate, others find it at the bottom of a carton of ice cream. There are many who find satisfaction through partaking in recreational drugs, some find it through the art of making love. Elise Conroy carved out her path to satisfaction, and today it was going to be through watching Gregory Langston's reaction to what she placed on the windshield of his car: a strategically-highlighted copy of Sapphire's phone records, a photo of Sapphire hugging Zachary McFadden, and an letter which read:

G. Langston,

I know you are wondering who has anonymously been sending you information lately. Know that my identity is of no consequence as the information that I have been providing to you is of much greater importance. You can consider me a friend who has been looking out for your best interests. Sapphire Taylor is toxic. I wanted to spare you the pain, but I see that you need further proof of how toxic she is. I want you to think about something. Over the past few weeks, have you ever been with her on a Tuesday between the hours of 12 to 2pm? Check her phone records. Look at who she always places a call or text message to (which is highlighted). One could only assume she partakes in her acts of debauchery during those hours. I even enclosed a photo of the two of them in a loving embrace. I hope that further helps to solidify in your mind the kind of woman she is. I sincerely hope that this doesn't hurt you too badly. I'll leave you to examine the new information I've given you.

Sincerely,

A Friend

P.S.

You may want to begin questioning whether or not the child she was carrying was in fact yours. It's just another bit to mull over.

Watching from afar, Elise studied Gregory as he walked to his car in the parking lot designated for university staff. He peered at the envelope on his windshield, grabbed it, and sat in his car reading the contents. The look on his face caused a smile to form on Elise's. His face began to contort and his chest began to rise and fall in quick succession. Suddenly, he threw the papers away from him in a fit of rage and his fists began to pound upon the steering wheel. After seeing that her mission was accomplished, Elise shifted her car into drive and began her ride home. The smile of a happy woman was etched across her face. *That was better than an orgasm*, she thought to herself. Today Elise tasted satisfaction, savored its juices, and yearned for more.

CHAPTER 39

Sapphire was no stranger to hard drink. She enjoyed indulging in beverages that would keep her mind from focusing on thoughts that would send her into deep, dark places…places that would shatter lesser individuals. She knew her relationship with Gregory was going to end, but she wanted the pleasure of knowing that she, not he, would be the one to initiate the relationship's demise. She lost control. How could she lose control of a situation to a man? A man having the upper hand in any aspect of her life was unacceptable. He had to be taken down a peg or two. Gregory would not have the last laugh…at least not at her expense. She would ensure that she had the upper hand, no matter what.

Leaving Gregory's office, Sapphire decided to drive to The White Orchid, an upscale eatery where those who are known to be more affluent go to relax, conduct business meetings, and indulge in the city's famous Mai Tai bar. A finely-dressed gentleman host escorted Sapphire to a booth in the bar area. Although the host offered Sapphire several menus, she only took the drink menu while scanning the sea of patrons sitting at the bar. At first, she only concentrated on the male patrons, trying to spot any eligible men that she could throw her feminine wiles toward. As far as the women, she quickly glanced at them to size up her competition. None could compete with her beauty. Sapphire smirked to herself.

"I'm in here with a sea of dogs," she chuckled out loud.

"Excuse me?" the host asked for clarification.

"I'm sorry. I was just talking to myself."

"I'd like to introduce myself. I'm Pablo, and I'd like to welcome you to The White Orchid. I see you have our drink menu and I hope that you find your experience here a pleasurable one. I can make many suggestions as to what would be a fine drink, but if you have something in mind, I can bring that right to you."

"I'd like the White Orchid Mai Tai, and keep them coming. I don't want an empty glass. Make them heavier on the rum. You understand?"

"I do. I'll be right back with your Mai Tai."

"Thank you."

Sapphire loved the way the staff at the restaurant catered to her. This was indeed the distraction she needed to get her mind off of the contentious meeting she left no more than an hour ago. The establishment was alive with banter from the city's elite. As busy as The White Orchid was, Sapphire found it to be calming. This calm allowed her to hatch the perfect plan about how she would handle Gregory. Enjoying her sixth Mai Tai, feeling buzzed, Sapphire scanned the room again. This time she noticed a very distinguished, middle-aged White male having a drink with a woman she didn't notice before. *Maybe I do have some competition in this joint,* Sapphire thought studying the interaction between the two. She noticed how the two would smile, laugh, and review what appeared to be important documents. They sipped on various drinks, and finally the woman signed the check. *That bitch is dumb as hell. How the fuck is she going to be paying for a White man's drinks?* Sapphire thought, sucking her teeth.

After the woman signed the check she got up, shook the man's hand, and exited out of sight. Sapphire, feeling the weight of all of the drinks she consumed, felt a sudden rush of bravado. *I'll show that bitch how to mold a man!* she thought as she walked over to where he was sitting. Once she was a few feet away from his table and in his line of vision, she purposely dropped her keys.

"How clumsy of me..." she laughed while bending over and slowing picking up her keys.

"Clumsy or not, I'm glad you did that near me."

"If I didn't know any better, I'd say you were flirting with me."

"Then you'd be right."

"Then why don't you offer me a seat and tell me your name?"

"By all means, please, have a seat. I'm Michael Matthews."

"I'm Sapphire, like the gem, but much more valuable," she introduced herself with a chuckle.

"If you don't mind me saying, you're far more beautiful than any sapphire I've ever seen."

"Thank you very much."

Michael and Sapphire conversed for an hour exchanging compliments, giving commentaries about pop culture, and simply enjoying each other's company. Sapphire continued to consume more alcohol as she tried to convince Michael, as well as herself, that she was the gem that he needed in his life in order to be 'whole'.

"How are you getting home tonight?" he questioned.

"Why? Are you offering me a ride?"

"No…I'm asking because I'll call you a cab; you've had way too much to drink," Michael retorted.

"I thought you liked gems."

"I do, but I like my job more. Sapphire, beginning tomorrow I'll be managing this place, and I don't want to start going home with the second most beautiful woman I've met in here today."

"Second? You must be talking about that woman I saw you with earlier," Sapphire concluded, feeling rejected. "Well you know what? You couldn't handle this any fucking way! The least you could do is spot my check!" she said getting up, leaving him where he was sitting.

Sapphire stumbled to the powder room to splash water on her face. She knew that she needed to drive home and getting caught driving drunk was not an option. After patting her face with a towel, she poured herself a cup of complimentary coffee and sat on the lavish couch. The room was heavily adorned with white silk orchids. Sapphire, even in her state of intoxication, couldn't help but be fascinated by the room's beauty. While trying to regain her bearings, the woman who was previously sitting with Michael walked through the door.

Immediately, Sapphire made her disdain for the woman known by sucking her teeth and rolling her eyes.

"I'm sorry, young lady. Is there a problem?"

"Did I say there was a problem?"

"Well from looking at you; clearly you've had too much to drink."

"Mind your fucking business."

"I'm sorry. I was just trying to be helpful. I walk in here to see a woman with terrible posture, slumped over the couch, who reminds me of the trash my husband was sleeping with." The woman paused, looking at Sapphire from head to toe. "Yeah, you look just like her. See, my husband was cheating on me with a young woman who looked just like you. Trash!"

"What did you say to me, bitch?" Sapphire started, but the woman interrupted her tirade.

"She was a woman with no moral fiber whatsoever. I know her type. A WMD: Weapon of Mass Destruction! Women like her do nothing but seek out married men; they have no concern for the families that are destroyed in their wake. I feel sorry for women like that."

Stumbling closer to the woman, slurring her words, Sapphire hissed, "Bitch, you don't even know me. You can't even get a White man to pay for your drinks."

"You've called me a bitch one time too many. Honey...look in the mirror - you're a mess!" The woman stepped back and smiled with contempt, "Mmmm...you do look like her, but you aren't her. She was put together much better than you. This girl looked like she had class, and obviously that's not a quality you possess. Don't find your way back into this establishment again. We don't cater to your type."

"You don't own this place. I'll come here as often as I want..." Sapphire began but she was interrupted yet again by the woman.

"On the contrary, sweetie...everything in this establishment I own, I designed, hand-picked, and paid for. Over the years, let's just say I had a lot of time to invest in this place and recently I decided to make my presence a permanent fixture here. So if you want to avoid the embarrassment of having the police escort you off the premises, I suggest you get your drunk, tacky, sloppy ass out of here."

The woman turned around and left Sapphire standing alone in the powder room. As the woman made her way to exit The White Orchid, she stopped by Michael's table. "I know you're not officially starting until tomorrow, but she's in the bathroom. Make sure she leaves without making a scene."

"You got it, Mrs. Langston."

"That's Ms. Langston." She replied with a chuckle.

CHAPTER 40

The clatter of Joan's Valentino floral mesh sandals were heard as she made her way down the hall to enter the office of Principal Mackenzie. Joan hated the fact that she had to take her daughter out of school, but she was left with no choice.

"I wanted to meet with you personally to issue my apologies for taking Anna out of school today. I know you were counting on her to deliver in today's debate against Cedar Hall, but I'm sure you can find a replacement. An emergency has come up, and I need her to come with me immediately."

"A student of Anna's talents is indispensible, but we'll make the adjustment. I hope everything does work out, Mrs. Langston. I appreciate your coming in and letting me know about Anna's absence in person."

"It's the least I can do," she smiled, rising to shake his hand.

"I'll have Kathleen call Anna down for you."

"Thank you so very much," Joan said while exiting the room.

Principal Mackenzie noticed that there was something considerably different about Mrs. Langston during her visit. She didn't wear an air of nervousness, but rather one of confidence. While Mrs. Langston was beautiful before, now her beauty seemed to dazzle. Was it the fact that she was dressed from head to toe in Valentino? Was it the fact that even though she was picking up her daughter for an emergency that she still seemed happier than when he last saw her? Whatever it was, the change was considerable and palpable. Shaking his head, but smiling to himself, he pressed a button on his phone to call his secretary, Kathleen. "Please call Anna Langston's classroom; she's being dismissed for the day. Then call Angela McFadden. We need her to fill in for Anna in the debate against Cedar Hall…" Principal Mackenzie paused for a moment to think and then continued. "No, never mind about Angela. She's been distracted lately…better yet, call Devin Horsley."

"I hate to pull you out of school, but we have to act fast."

"What's going on?"

"It's Jonathan."

With growing excitement and nervousness, Anna asked, "What about Jonathan?"

"I know you love him and he loves you. If I didn't feel, with every

"I know he hasn't. What does that have to do with Jonathan?"

"Last night while your father was sleeping, I decided to do some digging of my own. You know your father's ego makes him truly believe that he is the smartest man alive. His ego is so inflated that he doesn't even think I have the foresight to check his phone. Additionally, he doesn't even have a passcode to access his voicemail. I heard his phone vibrating, so I decided to give it the old college try. That cocky bastard didn't even wake up. So when I tried his voicemail, you wouldn't believe my shock when I discovered how easy it was to listen to his messages."

"No!"

"It gets worse. If the saved messages from his mistresses weren't enough, the message from a private investigator was enough to tell me that we have to act, and I mean act now. I played the message again on speakerphone and recorded it with my phone's voice memo function so that I could save the message on my phone. I then deleted the message on his phone as well as the missed call from the call log and placed his phone back in his pants pocket. Anna, you need to hear this for yourself. I'm sorry, baby."

Taking out her cell phone, she navigated her finger across several screens to finally play the message that would prove once and for all that evil does come in all forms:

Sorry to be getting back to you so late. When you called me I was in the middle of a lap dance with two fine bitches. You can understand that huh, Greg? The man burst out into uncontrollable laughter, then continued. *Hey, I been trying to dig up as much as I could on that spick, but his fingers are clean. He got a clean family, no arrests...nothing. He don't even gotta fucking parking ticket on record. The only way we can take him down is to prove he's been sleeping with your daughter when she was 16. So, the statutory rape angle you were considering is your best bet. You did say she was 16 years old when they got together, right? You better do it now if you're going to do it. Will she be leaving for school this fall? Get back to me.*

The two sat silent for a moment. After processing that her father would be callous enough to have the man she loved arrested for statutory rape and thinking about how his life would be ruined for simply loving her was more than she could bear. Her mother was a far better actress than she was. "This shit ends tonight!" an enraged Anna professed.

"Agreed..." Joan concurred shaking her head.

CHAPTER 41

A very wise woman once said, "Don't let your left hand know what your right hand is doing." Wiser words could not have been spoken regarding Mrs. Joan Langston. Early on in her marriage, when her mother was still living but gravely ill, she was told one thing that resonated with her. Those words remained with her until now. "Baby, when you become a mother, you're going to see that there will be times when you may get lost in trying to be a good wife. Shit, we all fall victim to that at some point or another, but being a mother means that you have a responsibility greater than self. God endows us with the gift to give life, and that means you have to ensure by all means necessary that Joan will be okay. I like that Greg. He's fine and he got potential. But make sure that if there is no Greg, there is a Joan."

Joan, reclining in her office chair, dialed seven digits on her cell phone. "Are you ready?"

"Yes."

"It has to happen tonight."

"Once it's done then we part ways and cease communication for good."

"I have no problem with that."

"So we're understood?"

"With crystal clarity…" Joan replied stoically. Both parties hung up their respective phones and threw them in the garbage.

Anna, while driving in her car, felt an intense level of anxiety swell within her. Every red light she encountered prompted her to apply her right foot to the break. Each idle moment ignited increasing thoughts of a life that was, in many respects, made stronger by an overbearing father; but in some respects, her life was also made worse. She thought about how she felt so little personal joy in her life. When she honestly reflected over her short life, she realized that she spent most of it trying to please a man who viewed her accomplishments as something to criticize rather than praise; not meeting standards was blasphemous. She found joy with her mother and in the loving relationship she forged with Jonathan; now her father threatened to secretly destroy that. His actions proved that he cared nothing for the happiness of her mother. Anna, having been raised a Langston, luckily possessed the best qualities of both of her parents. As she arrived at her destination, she thought, *this has to be done.* She reached over and pulled latex gloves out of the glove compartment.

As the darkness of night cloaked the city, Anna could see Sapphire arriving home. *Okay, one hour then it's time*, she said to herself. Anxiously watching the clock on the dashboard, an hour later she stepped out of her car and proceeded to cross the street. Walking steadily toward the townhouse door, Anna took a deep breath, and then pressed the doorbell. She waited for a moment and then pressed it again. Moments later the door opened. "What the hell are you doing here?" Sapphire questioned, recognizing Anna from a photo Professor Langston kept in his office. "You've got some fucking nerve coming to my home unannounced!" her voice rose, and her agitation grew more and more by the second. Before another word could be uttered by Sapphire, Anna stepped aside and another familiar face stepped forward and thrust a knife into Sapphire's chest and abdomen in several swift, consecutive motions.

As Sapphire fell to the floor, Anna and the unnamed guest left as quickly as they had arrived. She was unable to scream and unable to move. Sapphire, stretched on the floor of her townhouse in her own blood, could think of one thing and one thing only. Her waning thoughts were on the one person she loved in life, and that was Ms. Strickland. She began to think about the life Ms. Strickland wanted for her and she felt flushed with a sense of shame. She could hear a faint voice calling her from the distance, *Baby, you can't come home to me like this; not like this.* Sapphire's breathing grew increasingly shallow until they stopped completely.

"Joan! Joan! Come down here! I have to tell you what's happened, it's important!" Leaving his car engine running and the door ajar, Gregory yelled as he ran into the house in a panic. Running up the stairs, he ran to the bedroom to see the television and lights on, but he found no one. "Joan! Joan! Where the hell are you?" Gregory yelled as he frantically checked each room of his estate that had a light on.

Sirens could he heard from a distance, only adding to the frenzy inside the Langston estate. Outside, Joan reached inside Gregory's car to retrieve a perfectly-crafted letter addressed to him written in Anna's handwriting. She handed it to her daughter. "I'll take care of it," her only child said.

Leaving the Langston estate as a passenger, Anna informed the driver of the vehicle to drop her off at the park on 12th street and Laurel Avenue. "I know we won't talk after this, but I want you to know, and this comes from both my mother and me, we're sorry for your loss."

"It's okay. Everything finds a way of working itself out in the end."

The contents of the bag: latex gloves, the confession letter, and the knife used to murder Sapphire would be disposed of by Anna - her knowledge of forensics would now be coming in handy. The cloak of night proved to aid Anna in her endeavor. A trash receptacle was located in the center of the park and Anna placed the bag of evidence inside with the exception of the knife. Using a large umbrella to shield herself and the trash can from the rain, she poured an accelerant onto the bag and lit a match. She watched the proof burn and the walked away.

Breaking News:

University Professor Gregory Langston has been arrested for the murder of one of his students: Sapphire Taylor. Police officials have indicated that he has confessed to murdering her, but he later attempted to recant his story by stating that he was covering up for his daughter. Langston told detectives that he even had a letter proving his claims, however, when homicide detectives searched his car, they found no such letter. Moreover, sources are exclusively reporting to Channel 8 that Sapphire Taylor and Langston are said to have had an adulterous relationship. More details at 11.

EPILOGUE

The Langston women navigated rocky seas over the past several years, however, both found a way to persevere and rise above their troubles. Anna, while driving home from Rhode Island with Jonathan, was looking forward to sharing with her mother that she yet again ended her sophomore year at Brown on the Dean's List. Additionally, she wanted to surprise her mother by showing her the 12 carat diamond ring from Tiffany's she proudly wore on her index finger.

Jonathan's success as a mortgage broker afforded him the ability to live a life not concerned with finances. Brokering the deal on the casino expansion ensured his financial stability. He also had a knack for wisely investing his finances. His life revolved around Anna and increasing his net worth so that one day they and their future children would forever be comfortable. Jonathan not only told Anna that he loved her but he showed her daily.

Packing her bags to take a long overdue vacation, Joan smiled as she thought to herself, *Jason and Chris are going to flip when they see this outfit. What happens in Vegas damn sure better stay in Vegas!* She decided to take a two week vacation in Vegas to celebrate the publication of her new cookbook and the expansion of The White Orchid. Ms. Joan Langston also had another reason to celebrate: her divorce from Gregory had just been finalized. Freedom, personal wealth, and her best friends were engaged. Could life get any better? Yes, it could. When Joan received the news that her daughter was still holding a 4.0 GPA and was engaged to her Latin lover, she finally felt a wholeness that she didn't remember feeling - ever.

Elise Conroy returned to work, however, she never fully recovered from her mother's death. She acknowledged that she needed to seek professional help for her obsession with making Gregory Langston suffer, and she spent several months in therapy. The last she heard, Gregory was sentenced 7 to10 years for the death of Sapphire on the account that the conviction was circumstantial. Prosecutors couldn't conclusively prove that he killed her because there were no witnesses and no weapon was found. Elise still found pleasure in making sure that Cheryl's cousin, who happened to be serving time in the same prison, 'enjoyed' Gregory as much as possible. As time went on, Elise eventually became remorseful about killing Sapphire. She believed that it was unfortunate that Sapphire had to die, however, she was collateral damage. Gregory was the larger target and Sapphire was a means to an end. Again, Elise sought professional help, but was smart enough to never mention killing Sapphire; doctor-patient confidentiality only goes so far.

Professor Langston is serving a sentence for a crime he didn't commit. He found life in prison to be hell; it was a lot more miserable than he had ever imagined. He was accustomed to the privilege of the finest things in life: sleeping on plush beds with linens that had thread counts no less than one thousand. He dined in the finest restaurants and enjoyed partaking in joyous, indiscriminate sexual rendezvous with beautiful women. Now he was forced to live in an environment with the dregs of society who committed the most heinous acts. He had to eat meals that were devoid of flavor and were most certainly not prepared with the care and presentation that he was used to. He no longer had any sense of privacy; he was made to sleep in a cell that was quite unsanitary to say the least. Gregory found his manhood violated almost nightly, because the alternative was to face extreme brutality. Professor Gregory Langston, a man of intelligence that once had it all - now all he had was a plan. Over and over in his mind, he would repeat, *This was a set up...those bitches will pay...* Gregory knew he would be free one day and his first target would be his former wife, then the child who was too much like her...both women were nothing like the woman he was framed for killing.

One may admire precious gems in a showcase and never realize the painstaking process that a gem must go through in order to make it shine. Sapphire was very much like a gem in a showcase: gems can be appreciated from afar, but the second a gem cracks, the value is lost. The moment Sapphire's innocence was taken, she was never the same. Defense mechanisms and sexual promiscuity were used to shield wounds that never healed. At the end of Sapphire's life, with eyes closing in death, she remembered the words Ms. Strickland taught her when she was young from Deuteronomy 31:6: *Be strong and courageous. Do not be afraid or terrified because of them, for the Lord your God goes with you; he will never leave you nor forsake you.* She asked for God's forgiveness before parting this life and heard the welcoming voice of Ms. Strickland once again. The gem was broken no longer.

DISCUSSION QUESTIONS

- Which character do you empathize the most with?
- Do you view Sapphire more as a victim or a villain?
- Why do some women stay in unhealthy marriages (e.g., Joan)?
- What do you think about the dynamic of Joan and Jason's friendship?
- Do you believe that Joan is a good mother?
- What do you think of the age difference between
- Jonathan and Anna? Is it common? Should it be condoned?
- Do you know anyone as callous as Gregory?
- Who is the most complex character in Broken Gems?
- Is revenge ever justified? Think about Elise.
- Do you believe Gregory deserved what happened to him at the conclusion of the novel?

About the Author

TJ Haynes was born in New Haven, Connecticut. TJ is the youngest of five siblings. TJ attended Southern Connecticut State University, where he received a Bachelor's Degree in English. He later received his Master's degree in Education  from Walden University. He has one child, a daughter, and is currently a high school English Teacher. With an insatiable thirst for knowledge, TJ is currently enrolled at Sacred Heart University in Fairfield, Connecticut pursuing a post Master's degree in Educational Leadership.

TJ Haynes initially developed his love for writing while in high school. During those years he wrote numerous short stories and poems. "Writing was always so cathartic, especially during the most difficult times of my adolescence," TJ explains. When he initially began writing, he was rather shy about sharing his work with the public; however once he stepped out of his comfort zone and allowed others to read his work, the love and adoration he received came in abundance. The praise of those he allowed to read his early writings fueled his passion to continue on his path of one day being a published author.

While working on his undergraduate degree, TJ fine-tuned his writing of short fiction, and wrote prolifically. His love for the written word only increased and upon graduation. TJ used his love for writing in the classroom when he became an English Teacher; not only teaching American Literature, but Creative Writing as well. It was while teaching one of his creative writing classes that the conception of his first novel, Broken Gems was conceived. TJ notes, "Broken Gems initially started as short story I wrote and used to complement a lesson on character development. The response I received was overwhelming." The accolades from his students served as inspiration to turn Broken Gems into a full length novel. Additionally, the untimely passing of his beloved mother served to fuel his desire to bring Broken Gems to fruition, as the novel is dedicated to her memory.

While raising his daughter, teaching, and pursuing his Master's Degree, TJ Haynes channeled his creativity and wrote Broken Gems. For many years TJ longed for the day that he could call himself a published author, and tell a story that he always knew he had within him. TJ is currently planning to begin writing the sequel to Broken Gems.

CPSIA information can be obtained at www.ICGtesting.com
Printed in the USA
BVOW081600171012

303178BV00001B/19/P